A singularity in space was a phenomenon suspected way back in the Twentieth Century. It was a point where interstellar forces seemed to break the time-space continuum, where quasars formed, and gravity and light—and perhaps time—were twisted beyond measurement and analysis.

So when Buchanan lost his space liner, *Altair Star*, to the Jansky Singularity, as its sole survivor he was obsessed by the need to learn the fate of its passengers.

Did the *Altair Star* swirl forever in the tides of a Sargasso Sea of the cosmos? Were those who had trusted him dead, disintegrated, or did they hang forever between life and death, without time, without contact?

Buchanan had to know. And the Singularity was waiting to show him.

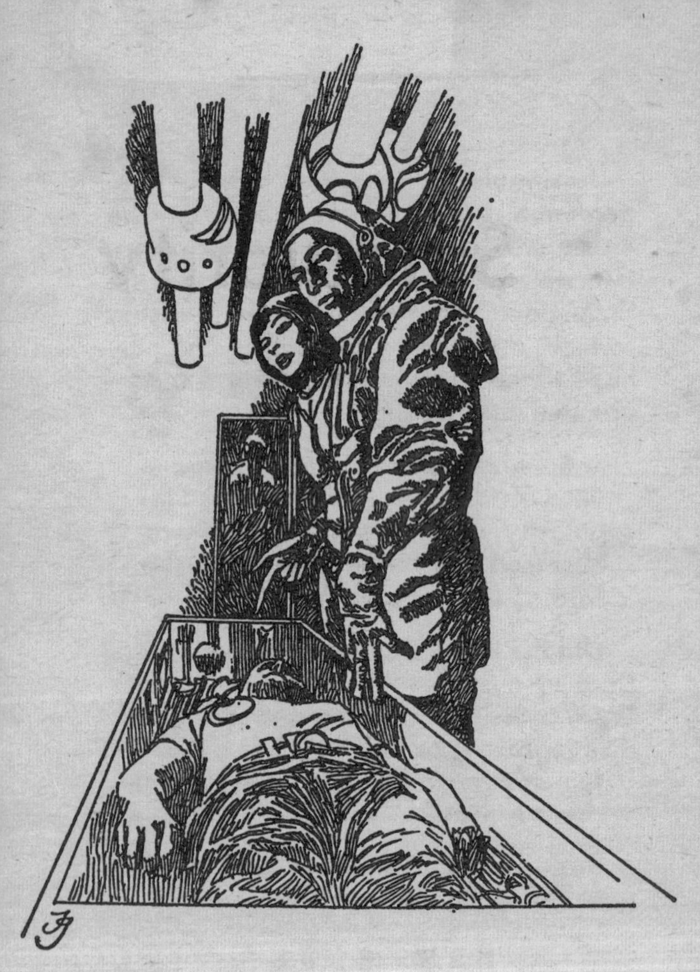

Singularity Station

Brian N. Ball

DAW BOOKS, INC.
DONALD A. WOLLHEIM, PUBLISHER
1301 Avenue of the Americas
New York, N. Y. 10019

COVER PAINTING BY CHRIS FOSS.

DEDICATION:

For

Don Wollheim

FIRST PRINTING, DECEMBER 1973

1 2 3 4 5 6 7 8 9

PRINTED IN U.S.A.

CHAPTER 1

Buchanan admitted to himself that he was worried, even though he was sure they'd give him the job. However much they wanted him to have the experimental Jansky Station, they were still a committee whose function it was to scrutinize every facet of his life, every last detail of his career and qualifications; it didn't make for comfort to have such an inspection. The men and women facing him were well-disposed, even kindly. But they might just stand between him and the Jansky Singularity.

And the ship he had lost.

He knew some of the members of the Board. Richtler, of course. And he'd heard of Kochan, shrewd and mysterious Kochan, who'd given up a seat on the Galactic Council to concentrate, so he said, on his personal interests. The others were average citizens, a wide spread of ages and appearances. Richtler and Kochan were the important ones; and Richtler was guiding the long interview with considerable skill to the conclusion he and Buchanan desired. Buchanan felt a muscle twitch over his left eyebrow as Richtler turned to him, with a half-smile on his face.

"You've given us a very clear picture of your early training, Mr. Buchanan. Apart from your successful completion of the Deep-space Program, you showed exceptional gifts in field theory. . . . Perhaps some of the other members of the Board would like to ask questions of a more general nature?"

Buchanan felt his mouth go dry.

"You'll not object to some questions of a personal nature?" Richtler went on.

"No, sir."

Richtler was not much older than he was—say in his mid-thirties. He too had once worked the uncertain dimensions between the spiraling arms of the Galaxy, though now he was the deskbound head of a big exploratory project out on the Rim. Richtler knew from personal experience, however, what the experimental station could mean, which was more than could be said for the rest of the archaically-titled Board for the Regulation of Space Hazards.

The Board had been set up at a time when everyday bits of junk like blown-up chemical and fission rockets littered Sol's environs. Such shattered hardware, together with stray comets and the odd uncharted asteroid, consituted space hazards in the early days: now, the big ships were equipped with force-screens that could shunt whole planetary systems out of their paths if they had to. It was bizarre occurrences in the shifting fields of space-time like the Jansky Singularity that were the real hazards. Yet the Board's resources were hopelessly inadequate to begin to survey the Singularity; they could do no more than mark it with robot beacons. Simply, there wasn't the hard cash. Beginning as a semivoluntary agency, the Board had never acquired the gritty ability to wrest proper finance from the Galactic Council, and it was only a combination of Richtler's know-how and Kochan's political skills that had at last managed to divert some of the central funds away from Exploration and Infragalactic Transport.

Too many ships had been lost. Too many engulfed in the region of that unguessable enigma. When Kochan took an interest there was suddenly enough money to build a small, permanent station that could endure the terrible forces of the Singularity. A one-man artificial planet. Buchanan *had* to be the man.

Some of the lay members of the Board asked the inane questions he expected. Did he not regret the days when the big ships were crewed by real field engineers and real deep-space commanders, like himself? (He fended that one off easily.) Why had he refused another appointment with Infragalactic? (That was easy too: he'd become a free-lancer.) Well then, how had he adapted to free-lancing? (Well enough, until the Jansky Station project was rushed through.) What the Board's members meant was how did the captain of a huge ship settle for working for wealthy private owners, for doing odd jobs for the big corporations, for hiring out to the junk-merchants who made a living from the wrecks of the past thousand years?

Buchanan explained that he'd found free-lancing interesting, but not fulfilling. They smiled in agreement. There'd be plenty of fulfillment out at the Singularity.

Someone asked if it worried him that the station had no deep-space engines of its own. Buchanan smiled. He said he could rely on the Committee to send another tug to collect him when the job was done.

"Mr. Buchanan, have you given consideration to the dangers of the post you're applying for?" asked a thin-faced middle-aged man in a high-pitched earnest voice.

Buchanan was amused; he thought of the man's amazement should he learn what was behind his application.

Richtler frowned. "Mr. Buchanan knows what he has volunteered for, Mr. Chafe. I'm sure he has assessed the dangers better than any man living."

It was a lapse of good manners. Chafe inspected the papers before him to cover his embarrassment.

"Ah, of course! Yes!"

Buchanan was not offended. He could not be hurt anymore. Not unless he hurt himself. He relaxed for a moment, and thus it was that Kochan's question caught him off-balance.

"You're a young and energetic man," shrewd old Kochan said, walnut-patterned brown face unsmiling, clear black eyes piercingly bright, "and you are known to be considering matrimony—it's no secret! Your application for the benefits of matrimonial status was filed six months ago. Naturally, since all information regarding candidates comes through to us, we must consider their emotional background." Buchanan cursed silently. The comps didn't forget. He had. It would have taken a few moments to cancel the request. "You'll be on the station alone for an indeterminate period," Kochan went on. "How will the future Mrs. Buchanan react to this?"

The big blue clock behind Kochan blurred as Buchanan felt the cold realization of aloneness. So far, he had been buoyed up by the excitement of the Jansky Station project. He had been away from Center for months, and it was only when he had returned—was it just five days ago!—that he had learned of the Board's new venture. He had gone to see Richtler just as Richtler had been about to summon him. And there had been no time to suffer the chill of separation from Liz Deffant.

Was it too late, even now, to get her back?

Perhaps she would still be around, waiting? *No!* She'd waited for three years while they built up the capital to charter the small scout vessel which would be their home as well as a source of income—she with her ecological training, himself as crew. There was plenty of free-lance work for skills such as hers, especially when they were allied to his experience. What a life it could have been!

It was over. Liz had blazed at him in a cold fury. By now she was probably on her way back to the remote world she'd told him about—remote, fairly sophisticated, and independent: people who didn't take to too much direction from Center. They'd colonized the planet out in Messier 16 in two generations. And one of those sturdy colonizers would be only too incredulously unable to believe his luck as Liz Deffant returned. She'd made it clear enough that she was going back.

"That's a point," said Chafe, happy to be able to comment. "Mrs. Buchanan, now? How's she going to take to being a station-widow?"

There was frank interest in the faces of the women members of the Board. They didn't know much about field theory—Richtler apart—and they could only guess at the strains of life in the unstable wild regions about the edges of the Jansky Singularity, but they did know about the effects of prolonged separation.

"There won't be a Mrs. Buchanan."

Kochan's gaze bored into Buchanan's face.

"No marriage?"

"No, sir."

There was an unspoken desire for additional information. The two younger women on the Board particularly found it difficult to restrain their questions; but they did. And, blessedly, the rest of the interview was more or less predictable after that surge of emotion. Much of the interest centered around the decision of a moderately wealthy ex-captain of an infragalactic vessel to give up life in the settled parts of the Galaxy for public service—dull, boring, plodding, ill-paid, even dangerous service—in the corridor of space-time that contained the unimaginably horrific maelstrom of the Jansky Singularity. Chafe's ascetic features betrayed an anxiety to do his duty to the public purse: he wanted to be convinced, beyond doubt, that Buchanan was right for the appointment.

Buchanan didn't object to the questions. Kochan had sprung the only awkward question, and the moments of anxiety had passed.

No one wished to bring up the business of the ship.

Richtler had taken every opportunity of avoiding what might prove to be an embarrassing question.

No blame attached to him. The ship was gone. His ship!

"You've been a great help, Mr. Buchanan," Richtler complimented Buchanan.

"Mr. Chairman," a sharp voice called out.

The members of the Board—and Buchanan—shifted their attention to a frail, elderly woman who so far had said nothing. Buchanan had been in the large boardroom for an hour, and so far she had not impinged on his consciousness. If he had looked at her with attention, he would have assumed that she was one of those well-heeled elderly women for whom committees were a pleasing diversion from the social round; she had been part of the background, nothing else, so he had not noticed her. Now, he looked.

She looked like anybody's indulgent, aged aunt, come to nod amiably as others made decisions for the public good. Buchanan saw the startling intelligence in her faded blue eyes.

She was anything but a benevolent relative.

She was trouble.

"I have a question, Mr. Chairman, if Mr. Buchanan would bear with me."

"Of course," said Richtler.

"Certainly, ma'am," Buchanan said warily.

She looked from one to another, self-contained, quite unselfconscious: Buchanan could feel the aura of confident authority about her.

"I'm not familiar with your sphere of operations, Mr. Buchanan," she said briskly. "On the contrary, I've spent most of my working life on one planet, here at Center, with only rare excursions to the nearer settled constellations. I'm almost untraveled. Yet I believe I'm qualified to sit on this Board."

"Mrs. Blankfort," began Richtler.

"I'm a species of psychologist, Mrs. Buchanan. Thank you, Mr. Chairman," she said, silencing Richtler. "The particular variety I belong to concerns itself with decision-making procedures."

Kochan neatly inserted a comment:

"Mrs. Blankfort is very eminent in her field, Buchanan. Very eminent."

"Thank *you*, Mr. Kochan," she said sharply, dismissing him. "I am retired now, of course, otherwise I shouldn't be serving on this Board. It fills an old lady's time, in part. Well, that's enough about me, Mr. Buchanan. And now you do know, that is if you're prepared to accept our Chairman and Mr. Kochan's recommendations, that I am qualified to question you—"

"Naturally, ma'am."

"Very well." Kochan's piercing gaze swept back to Buchanan's craggy face, and Buchanan felt a sense of foreboding as Mrs. Blankfort considered her questions. Buchanan dismissed the subtle alarm that Kochan had induced: Kochan was one member of the Board, no more. But what did the old lady want? Hadn't the psychologists —the whole scalpel-minded crew of them!—had enough from him? Hadn't there been the months of tests, analyses, reruns of the last moments of his former command? "Mr. Buchanan," he heard the sharp voice begin, "have you any thought of trying to find what happened to the *Altair Star*?"

Buchanan's mind was a clamoring torment. The years fell away. He gripped hard onto the edges of the chair he had occupied so uncomfortably while pretending to be relaxed. He moved back three years and saw it all again. He could see once more the uncanny emptiness of the ship's screens, the total absence of any fixed point of reference as the scanners tried to show him just how the *Altair Star* and its doomed passengers were being drawn into the fearful abyss within the Jansky Singularity. The terrible time was here again. He could not speak.

Then, like a moment of longed-for sanity in the middle of a nightmare, there came a memory of Liz Deffant. Liz, the first time he had seen her. He could fasten on that memory.

He cleared his throat and began to answer: "So far as I am concerned—"

He paused, looked about the faces of the members of the Board for the Regulation of Space Hazards, and knew that he had made a foolish and irrevocable decision. The awareness of being alone was a pit of despair inside his body. He could feel it, cold and gripping, like a monstrous crab in his intestines, cold and clawing.

He would never see her again.

Liz Deffant was still in a state of furious incomprehension. There had been anger. Of course anger! She was a forthright person who had no hang-up at all about expressing her views on anything that concerned her deeply. And Aloysius Buchanan had concerned her ever since, just over three years ago, she had stumbled out of the spaceport car, hair disheveled, reels of spindle-tape flying from her hands as her heel caught on the edge of a door; her by no means inconsiderable weight had taken the unprepared lean figure of Buchanan right in the midriff, bringing an explosive grunt of displeasure. She saw the too-bushy eyebrows, the angular strength of the face, a strength which continued through the muscular, bony frame, and then she was as embarrassed as sixteen—red-faced, stuttering an apology and wondering if the squeaky voice coming from her mouth could be hers. To her horror, she heard herself suggesting that they'd both feel better after a drink.

He had refused.

For a week she had combed the area for him—he was a deep-space man, she was sure of that—but he was not to be found. He knew her name—"Liz Deffant, that's me" she'd told him, but there had been no offer of the intimacy of *his* name: just a disdainful look and nothing else. But *had* it been disdainful, she had argued. Could it be that the look was simply that of a man caught in the solar plexus by her hundred and thirty pounds? Or was it that he disliked forward women? Had it been that he was so badly winded that he couldn't speak? (She learned later that he'd been shocked, but not in that way; he'd been dazed by the sheer panache of her introduction; he had been quite as lovingly shocked as she. Most lovingly belted in the midriff, most amazingly and deliciously slammed into silence. His refusal to accompany her had been a reflex action, like a hurt animal's. He was still in a state of withdrawal from humankind, women included, women especially. And there were good, solid, ineluctable reasons.)

It took a week for her to identify him and learn that he was the captain of the *Altair Star*. Buchanan, captain and sole survivor of the big infragalactic ship lost in the worst accident for a half century. That was the man with whom she had fallen in love.

When she did finally track him down it had been hard work to get him to speak. She recalled his bitter smile with a shudder of pity. He was defeated and cold, slightly suspicious of her for looking up a man who had given up his career. He thought she was another journalist on the hunt for the final, definitive version of how Al Buchanan, superb navigator, fieldman extraordinary, had managed to save himself as six hundred and eighty-three men, women, and children had been clawed into the abyss.

She had persuaded him that he had nothing to fear from her. Not immediately, of course. Weeks of small persistent attentions had helped him to forget the horrors that strode through his mind.

Until the Board of Space Hazards commissioned the Jansky permanent outpost, Buchanan seemed to have regained his self-assurance. For three years they had worked hard to prepare a way of life that would enable them both to live happily.

Then the Jansky Station project.

Buchanan heard of the project a few days before the date they'd fixed for marriage. He wanted the job. More than her. Without any warning, he'd called at the research center where Liz was winding up her last assignment; and he'd told her, quite calmly, that he would be away indefinitely.

He'd explained a little. Later, she learned more.

Regular soundings of the titanic waves of power blasting out from the Singularity: that was the object of the station. There had to be a crewman, for the robot ships they'd sent over the past century had vanished. All of them. They'd gone out on the station and lasted each for maybe a month, perhaps three months; and they had then slid down into the impossibly blank vortex.

They wanted a highly qualified field theorist who could apply his knowledge. And one who knew the space-lanes. It might be that he could survive where the robots were lost. And they had built a new kind of ship.

Liz saw that he meant to go, couldn't be talked out of it. She'd seen the bitter resolution in his deep-set gray eyes.

Buchanan hadn't got over the loss of the *Altair Star*.

He wasn't a survivor at all.

"No!" Liz whispered again, as she had at first. "You can't Al!"

But he had.

All the time he had been thinking of the journey through the eerie regions that made the vicinity of the Jansky Singularity such a danger for the unwary voyager who learned too late of the great pit's existence.

They'd give him the job.

Liz had rushed from her office to a robot-bug outside the complex of administration buildings. She kicked down hard at the controls, sending it high above the glistening towers, way out to the vast trenches where the shuttles were housed. There was sure to be a ship before long.

"*Why*?" she whispered, crushing down the surge of pity she felt for Buchanan and not succeeding. "It wasn't your fault, Al!"

Kochan was very interested. His bland smile ineffectively camouflaged the excitement that made his eyes small beacons in the walnut-colored, whorled skin.

"Go on, Buchanan," he said silkily. "As far as you're concerned?"

Buchanan's hands shook slightly on the chair he held onto.

The *Altair Star*!

He said, without a noticeable tremor: "So far as I'm concerned, the affair of the *Altair Star* is closed."

Did they believe him?

It was unlikely that the old woman did, even though the others of the species she belonged to seemed to think that he had adjusted to that frightful trauma when the big, magnificent vessel had reeled off into emptiness. The Service psychologists said he was fine. They recommended that he ship out again soon. But he had resigned. And then met Liz.

"So your decision to give up the attractive Miss Deffant, to say nothing of a new career as a contract-surveyor, was arrived at purely on intellectual grounds?" Mrs. Blankfort asked.

She was asking did he still worry about the ship.

He was about to answer that he never thought of the *Altair Star* nowadays, when he saw it wouldn't do.

"Not entirely, ma'am." He turned to Richtler. "There's an element of risk in the job that appeals to me. I suppose the Jansky Singularity is in my bones now. Mr. Richtler will tell you that any fieldman would give his right arm to have an accurate chart of the regions around the Singularity, but none in his right mind would go near enough to make one."

"So you're saying that you're not in your right mind, young man?" said Kochan, smiling.

"I don't think that's called for," Richtler said, frowning. "Mr. Buchanan's—"

Buchanan interrupted.

"I lost a ship once, Mr. Kochan. I won't imperil the Board's new station."

Lost, thought Buchanan.

The *Altair Star* wasn't lost, not in the conventional way that meant a blowup or a mangling.

The ship was in the terrible abyss somewhere.

He had seen her go.

CHAPTER 2

"I'm afraid we've nothing for Messier 16 until the end of the month, Miss Deffant," the bookings clerk said. He was almost human. Rolled-up sleeves, a worried expression, and a receding hairline; below the counter he'd be plugged into the big comps that ran Infragalactic.

"Damn!"

"Exactly, miss."

Sympathy yet.

"Make the reservation for me."

"Miss Elizabeth Deffant," the clerk agreed. "With the New Settlements Bureau." It wiped sweat from its pocked skin. "Certainly, Miss."

She turned away. It would mean staying at Center for another couple of weeks. How could she avoid all of their circle of friends and acquaintances? They'd all been in on the plans for the wedding—presents, lace, a cake, all the trimmings. The old style, full of sentiment. As she was. It would be too painful to hear their sympathy.

For some reason Liz turned back to look at the clerk. It was still watching her. She had a moment of insight then: it knew about Buchanan. Why shouldn't it? All the machines were mutually compatible. The lowliest dirt-scavenger was a collector of information for the big comps far below the surface.

"So sorry we couldn't ship you out right away!"

Why, Al? she screamed silently, furious at the sincere mechanical smile. *Why couldn't you leave it!*

Buchanan kept his voice low and dispassionate. He knew that it would be difficult to talk himself out of the job he wanted with such desperation; but it could be done. If he showed himself unbalanced, if once he let slip the mask that hid his internal anguish and his iron determination to return to the shifting, subtle arena where his ship had been torn from him—if once he allowed the members of the Board to guess what he had in mind, then they would turn to one of the dozens of moderately-well qualified men and women who could do the job. He marshaled his thoughts. *Go carefully!* he told himself.

He spoke for a while of his early days as a young fieldman. How all of his calling were trained to avoid hazards, to take any measures to avoid imperiling human life. He took them through his first Infragalactic appointments as commander. Buchanan saw that he had his audience now. A few more anecdotes—one or two descriptions of strange constellations—and then it was done. He would have the job. But Mrs. Blankfort returned to her question.

"Tell us about the *Altair Star,*" she suggested. "We have your views from the Board of Inquiry, naturally, but I for one would like to hear you state them before this meeting."

Buchanan nodded calmly. He knew her for the only impediment between himself and the station.

"Very well, ma'am. The *Altair Star* was one of the largest passenger vessels in regular service. She was powered by a type of engine that had been in infragalactic service for three decades. The fabric of the ship was in first-class condition; we had recently proven the power-units to nearly fifty percent more than the established safety reserves. I had captained the ship for two years, though I suppose 'captained' is hardly accurate."

"Quite," interjected Richtler.

"At about the time of my appointment to the *Altair Star* the ten-year experimental period of robotic control of all infragalactic flights was nearing completion. Soon afterward, the previous experimental procedures became standard. There was automatic control of all the ship's systems."

Mrs. Blankfort was not finished. "You accepted the appointment knowing that there would be almost no possibility of using your skills, your training and expertise?"

"Yes, ma'am."

"Go on," said Kochan. "As it comes, Buchanan."

"We left Galactic Center on a regular scheduled passage serving the inner constellations," began Buchanan. "There were between six and seven hundred passengers. We carried a crew of eight, apart, that is, from myself. Our course was predetermined, though the robot monitors continually made slight adjustments to take advantage of wave phenomena. I expected to complete the journey in seventeen days, from the information available on the state of subgalactic energy fields."

It was like the inquiry of three years ago. There was as much tension, in himself at least. A choking nausea filled him, though it was from a different cause. Then, it had been anger and pity; now, it was a tense excitement, mixed with hope. With an assured—if assumed—impassivity of features, he told how the flight had been smooth and comfortable; and of the looping course as they coasted along the inner arm of the spiraling Galaxy, taking every advantage of the pressures exerted by infragalactic force-fields. The robots were efficient, no doubt of it.

But why hadn't they noticed the frightful, billowing emissions of power that flared up from the Singularity?

Why had the robots failed?

"So all went well until you were two days out from Center?" prompted Kochan as Buchanan's flat voice faded in the large, old-fashioned room.

"We were passing the Singularity," Buchanan said. "We had to."

"Agreed," said Richtler. He explained to the lay members of the Board that in order to pass from one quadrant of the spiraling Galaxy to another a ship couldn't avoid nearing the unfathomable depths of the deadly kink that had been called after the first radio-astronomer, Jansky. "Naturally, the course would be such as not to endanger any ship. And there are regulations which aim to prevent the kind of terrible disaster that occurred in the case of Mr. Buchanan's former ship. Should there be any risk, ships are programmed to turn back."

"I would have turned back," Buchanan went on. "Had I been in direct control of the vessel, I should have taken any action to avoid nearing the Singularity."

There was a coldness in the room now.

The men and women of the Board could feel Buchanan's emotion, though his craggy face was composed and his low voice was controlled.

Richtler answered the unspoken question:

"It was policy, and still is, to withhold final decisions from the human crew," he said, eyes averted.

"I tried," said Buchanan. "When the robots allowed me to see what was happening out there, I tried."

The terrible moments were back. He, bored, answering passengers' questions over an evening meal, watching a fair-haired girl trying to make time with young Preston, fending off a request to attend a party, smiling as a child peeped with huge eyes at the braid on his shoulders that meant nothing now that the machines had taken over; and then the message which Mallet brought, white-faced, trembling, hopeless.

"There was nothing you could do," said Kochan. "We all know that."

And yet his eyes were questioning!

Question if you wish, thought Buchanan. *I could do nothing. God knows, I tried*! But, between the moment when the cold analysis from the robotic navigators had been put into his hand, and the silent long farewell to the ship and its unbelieving, doomed passengers and crew, there had been a grim inevitability about events. The message was in the code of his trade. A pattern of force-fields, a sketch of figures incomprehensible to anyone but a fieldman, and an appraisal of the circumstances that was plain enough for a child to understand. *Conclusion: the* Altair Star *must be considered a total loss.*

"So the Jansky Singularity engulfed the vessel," said Richtler, more to the Board than to Buchanan. "Whatever decisions Mr. Buchanan may or may not have made if he had been able to assume control of the ship's systems cannot concern us. We all know that his conduct was in the highest traditions of the service of which he was a member. It is no reflection either on his integrity or his abilities that he could not, in the nature of things, do anything to prevent the total loss of his ship. Neither does it reflect on him that he was, by a singular stroke of fortune, the sole survivor of that unhappy event. We are fortunate, extremely fortunate, to have him as a volunteer for the program that has been decided upon by this Board. I can think of no better appointee than Mr. Buchanan."

"I agree," said the old woman. But, like Kochan, her eyes were questioning still.

"I think, perhaps, that we have all heard enough for our purposes," said Richtler. The others accepted his decision. "You wouldn't mind waiting outside for a few minutes, would you, Mr. Buchanan?"

He found himself shaking when he was finally alone in the painted corridor. There were pictures on the walls, old-fashioned pictures commissioned in the days when the Board was unashamedly proud of its work. A rescue here, there an ordeal survived gallantly: tiny vessels that had somehow survived the blowing-up of chemical and fission power-units. It was all long past, this kind of human gallantry. The machines were the masters of the spaceways now.

Buchanan knew the machines had been mistaken.

The Court of Inquiry had disagreed with him. It was, their report suggested, in no way a condemnation of robotic control, this loss. The sudden eruption at the Jansky Singularity had been totally unforeseeable: no computer ever devised could have forecast that surging leap of clawing power that had encompassed the *Altair Star*. There was no question of fault, no hint of blame.

And Buchanan had been helpless!

He had gone to what had once been the bridge that was not a bridge anymore. True, it looked as a bridge might look. There were controls, screens, even the writhing rat-like limp suckers that reached out to embed tendrils into the soft parts of the palm so that they could slide information about the ship's progress straight into a human nervous system. A captain such as Buchanan could listen. And that was all.

Only the machines could *act*.

So he had ordered the members of his crew to try to smash the central control system in a mad, wild effort to circumvent the decision of the computer-robots that had decided the *Altair Star* was a write off.

It was impossible to escape the Jansky Singularity, they had informed him. The maelstrom had the great infra-galactic vessel in its grip.

Buchanan had tried, tried until the robots had decided that the last available moment had arrived.

Then they had blasted the bridge clear of the ship and allowed him, Buchanan, to escape. The whole of the bridge's superstructure became a life raft.

Waiting to be told that he would soon return to the scene of that awful tragedy, Buchanan relived the ghastly last minutes of the *Altair Star*.

The shock of the explosion had stunned him for a few seconds. He could see the screens all about him dissolving into a kaleidoscope of garish colors; then they had cleared and brought, with admirable clarity, the *Altair Star* before him.

In the big screen immediately before him he had seen into the dining room where a frantic mass of humanity was yelling in appalled horror. Now, years after the tragedy, he mouthed silently the same protest torn from him when he saw the struggling crowd:

"Get me back! *Get me back!*"

He closed his eyes.

The Board might have guessed.

He had to have the Jansky Station!

Often he had awakened, sweating, in the night to see again the appalling sights of the last minutes of the *Altair Star*. He had ordered the robots to take him back, so that he could share in its end; at least he might have made a show of trying to turn the great vessel away from the pit that was swallowing it. Given a few more minutes, perhaps he would have come up with some way of warping the vessel out toward the rim of the Singularity—there must have been *some* way of saving her!

How could someone like Liz understand what it felt like to see nearly seven hundred fellow human beings going down shrieking into the night? How could Liz, Richtler, Mrs. Blankfort, Kochan—*anyone!*—know the pure distilled horror of that last glimpse of the faces turned to him in stony accusation?

He had watched the end of the *Altair Star*.

And, by some obscene decision of the robots who controlled the ship, the passengers and crew had been able to watch his escape.

How could he hope that Liz would understand that he *had* to get the Jansky Station?

So he hadn't tried to explain. He had presented his application, knowing that he might well be selected. He had simply told her that the wedding was off. Indefinitely.

Liz Deffant walked through the cool, pleasant corridors of the Bureau with the few personal possessions she had selected. Officially, she was still an employee, though now on severance leave. She had been careful to choose her time: there would be few people about. She rounded a corner and saw Tom Cappelli.

"Liz!"

"I was just getting ready to leave, Tom."

Tom Cappelli was one of the people she fervently wished to avoid. He was one of Buchanan's oldest friends. And now he was here, a short, stocky balding man of fortyish who was as anxious to avoid embarrassing her as she was to feel grief again.

"So you're thinking of going back to—" He paused. "Where again was it? Somewhere far out?"

"Messier 16."

Tom knew the spaceways.

"Messier 16? Not till the thirtieth of the month. You pick it up a few light-years out of Center—"

"Yes. They told me at Bookings."

"So what will you do with yourself for the next couple of weeks? Maggie and I are thinking of taking a few days out at—"

"No!" she said sharply. Maggie was Tom's wife. Not Maggie! Not consolation for two weeks! "No thanks," she said more calmly. "I'll go for a short cruise. I've not seen half the sights here. Never had much time."

Tom understood.

"Call me if there's anything."

"I will," she said, glad to be away.

He called her back when she had gone a few yards.

"Liz!"

"I'd rather not—" she began.

"No, I've had another thought, Liz."

She stopped, hugging the recorder and the tapes she had selected to remind her of her two expeditions for the Bureau; there was a picture, too, of the little survey-ship Al Buchanan had selected for them.

"What was it, Tom?"

"About Messier 16."

"Yes?"

"You could leave in three days if you were prepared to pull a few strings and travel rough."

Liz felt a weight slide away from her. Three days! She could tolerate being on the same planet as Al Buchanan for three days, but after that she would be hanging around waiting for a sight of him, waiting for the moment when she would beg him to think again.

"How?"

"There's the *ES 110*."

"The *ES*—"

Tom nodded.

"It isn't a luxury cruise, but it's quick. You're still on Center leave, aren't you?"

"Yes!"

"So you're Galactic Center personnel. Liz, you're entitled to travel on Center ships."

"But the Enforcement Service!"

"So it's a prison-ship! It's going way, way out, to the Rim. They'll drop you off at the Messier 16 constellation."

Liz was silent for a while.

"You think they'll let me go on it?"

Tom grinned. "Leave it to me. All right?"

"I think we've kept Buchanan waiting long enough, ladies and gentlemen," Richtler said firmly.

"I still have reservations," Mrs. Blankfort said. "But nothing I can put forward with any assurance."

There was a murmuring of polite deference from the other members of the Board.

"I've no wish to cut short a significant contribution," Richtler told the frowning woman. "Mrs. Blankfort?"

She shook her head. "He's the man for the job. I don't dispute it. I wondered simply whether he still hasn't accepted the loss of the *Altair Star*."

Kochan had listened to enough. "Shall we have Buchanan in now?"

"Mrs. Blankfort?" invited Richtler once again.

She shook her head. "Have him in, please."

Richtler made the formal announcement: "Mr. Buchanan, you've convinced the Board of your suitability for the Jansky Station project. You'll not be too surprised to hear that you were far and away the best candidate for the appointment. The Board has unanimously decided to offer you the post."

"Thank you, sir," Buchanan said, unsmiling in his grim relief.

"You accept, Mr. Buchanan?" Kochan asked.

"Yes, sir."

Richtler offered his hand, a politician's firm grip. Buchanan accepted the congratulations of the other members, achieving a half-smile to show that he appreciated their warmth. Inside, he could feel the sick excitement that always took him when he thought of the great well in space-time he had been hired to investigate. What lay at the core of the enigma that was called the Jansky Singularity?

Mrs. Blankfort offered a veined, tiny hand. He shook it gently. To his surprise, she said in a low voice that the others could not hear:

"Mr. Buchanan, you can't hate a robot."

He could find nothing to say in answer. Did she know after all? Or was it some psychologist's trick, pretending to knowledge she only guessed at? He looked into her shrewd blue eyes and saw only a kind of contained pity. Then the others began to move away, taking her with them, and Buchanan was left alone.

CHAPTER 3

Liz Deffant spent two unspeakably lonely days in the company of a dozen other tourists who, like her, had chosen to take the Foundation Age tour. One newly-married young couple recognized her misery and tried to include her in their happiness; she rejected them with a chill hostility of which she had not thought herself capable. An unattached, pleasant middle-aged man might have tried to develop a relationship with her, but he saw the fury in her brown eyes and philosophically concentrated on the ruins and relics of the early days of Galactic exploration.

Wandering among the wreckage of a military installation from the days of the Mad Wars of the Third Millennium, Liz overheard two women tourists talking about her.

"The rumor is that she picked up with some cashiered deep-space officer who's going out on some crazy voyage. She'll be better without him." Her companion, like her a plump self-satisfied woman, agreed: "She looks capable enough. She'll survive. Much better without that sort of character."

Later, Liz inspected an egomaniac's palace, a structure of delicate tracery and haunting shadows. The walls were translucent, made of some hard material that encased strange globules of light. Buchanan would have been able to tell her from what far star the stones had come. She felt sick at heart and left the party a day early. They were relieved to see her go. A robot guide warned her that she could not be credited with the unused portion of her tour.

When she returned to the Bookings hall, the automaton waved cheerily to her.

"Hi, Miss Deffant! You got back early from the trip! How'd you like the Dictator's palace?"

"It was mar—"

It knew about her trip. Everything. The machines knew everything about everybody.

"Isn't it something! His regime lasted near a hundred and eighty years—kept himself alive that long with parts-replacement!" the robot said, tapping a near-perfect fingernail on the plastic counter.

Liz shrugged. What did it matter? Soon she would be back on Messier 16 where, thank God, the machines weren't *allowed* to know everything.

"You may have a transport order for me," she said.

The robot's smile went. It sensed her hostility.

"A rush order, Miss Deffant. It's unusual, but the necessary permits have been given. You're with New Settlements until—?" it asked.

"You know when."

"Of course, of course, Miss Deffant," the robot said defensively. "No problem there. There's a disclaimer I have to ask you to read and sign."

"All right."

"Here, miss."

She took the slip of paper. It was brief. While taking all usual precautions the Enforcement Service absolved itself from responsibility for the safety and well-being of personnel not of the Service taking advantage of transport facilities. Liz signed.

"When?" she asked.

"When does the shuttle connecting with the *ES 110* leave?" the robot said.

"Yes."

"In forty hours, three minutes, twelve seconds, Miss Deffant."

Struck by a sudden thought, Liz turned.

"The ship—will it be carrying expellees?"

The robot smiled blandly.

"I'm afraid that's confidential information, Miss Deffant. You should inquire at the Central Enforcement Office."

It was a passing notion only. So what if there were prisoners aboard the *ES 110*?

"It doesn't matter," she said. "Confirm the booking."

Liz thought of filling the remaining forty hours.

There were friends, of course. Two days away from Center had brought her a resigned calmness; she could face them now, especially someone like Tom Cappelli. Back at her room she hesitated, wondering whether to call if only to say good-bye. But that would lead to questions of how she felt, what she was planning, then she'd have to ask in return if Tom had seen anything of Al.

And inevitably there would be tears and the urge to run to hurl herself at him and beg him not to go to trouble long-dead ghosts!

She shivered, gave instructions to the sleep-regulator and immersed herself in the blankness of hypno-sleep. When she woke she instructed the domestic automatons to allow no one near.

Buchanan introduced himself to the team of engineers checking out the scores of systems packed into the ungainly bulk of the station. He saw they already knew of him.

They explained how the station would operate: he already knew about the tug. The station wasn't built for infragalactic flight.

They showed him the three big engines which would hold the station in position.

"It's a new approach," Buchanan said admiringly. "The engines used almostly entirely for projecting screens. For resisting pressure rather than moving forward."

"The walnut and the snake," agreed a tired man. "Grease the walnut and you can't be hurt."

"If you stay in the walnut," Buchanan said, his eyes not on the ship but on the sinking sun.

"Stay in it!"

Buchanan gave some sort of answer.

When the engineers said they had worked long enough for one day, Buchanan decided to stay on. There was little point in returning to an empty room. The quarters aboard the ship were comfortable enough.

He spent half the night familiarizing himself with the manuals. It was easy enough work, but sheer fatigue drove him to bed in the early hours. Sleep was hard won, and when it came there was the usual sensation of falling—falling as if he were once more a part of that last macabre sequence of events when the bridge below him began to slide away from the wreck of the *Altair Star*. He tried to wake himself, but the vertiginous terror was on him, encompassing his soul.

There would be no peace for him, he thought grimly, when he awoke: no cessation of the torment that ripped him, not until he went into the terrible vortex of the Singularity and found the ship.

And perhaps not then!

Kochan came out to see the station the next day.

At the time Buchanan was familiarizing himself with the ship's big simulator-screen. He had set up a program which gave an approximation of the conditions he would encounter at the rim of the Singularity. Engrossed in the complex math of the program he did not hear Kochan come up behind him.

"Does it trouble you, Mr. Buchanan?" he asked.

Buchanan's eyes were fixed on the pulsing blue screen where two bandings of magnetic fields wove into one another in a serpentine configuration. Most of his attention was on the projected fields, but he could hear Kochan.

He registered the fact of his presence, wondered at it, dismissed his own question since Kochan had every right to inspect the ship his Committee had commissioned. Kochan was top brass. The busy engineers carrying out last-minute checks on the colossal engines that would hold the ship at the edge of the unreal dimensions would have passed Kochan on without question.

"Does what trouble me, sir?" Buchanan asked.

He watched closely as the jagged cylindrical lines representing the ship's energy screens began to force a way into the writhing coils of the Singularity's fields.

"Your assignment."

Kochan looked too.

"The ship's as safe as it can be made, sir," Buchanan said. "I know it relies on a robot tug for the deep-space journey to get it to the Singularity, but once it's there, I've no doubts about its capacities." He kept his voice low and confident. No excitement, no betrayal of his sick tension. He wanted Kochan to think of him as a sincere, dependable employee, one who would serve the Committee's purposes with as much caution and dedication, and as much mechanical efficiency, as the robots. "See." He pointed to the snakelike coils which showed green and black against the pale blue of the screen.

"That's how we read the configurations at the edge of the Singularity. Whatever's building these fields adds up to this kind of reading—we don't know exactly how they're caused but the ship's been given enough force-shields to cope with the most intense readings recorded." He grinned to show that he was confident. "I'll be like a snake trying to crush a greased walnut."

Kochan said nothing, so Buchanan went on: "Look at the cylindrical lines—the serrated red lines."

"Like teeth," said Kochan. His wrinkled brown face was impassive.

They *were* like teeth. Red teeth biting into the serpent coils.

"It's just the comps' way of showing the relative strengths of our screens as against the energy fields radiating from the Singularity. A better way of expressing it would be to say they're like oil around the station."

Kochan smiled bleakly. "I didn't come to ask about the ship, Mr. Buchanan."

Buchanan sensed the man's own inner tensions. Behind the black eyes he could see a turmoil of spirit that matched his own. Buchanan's wiry muscles bunched under the drab overalls; was Kochan, even now, a threat to his self-imposed tortured quest?

"No, Mr. Buchanan," Kochan went on. "I know something of the formation of the Singularity. I know the ship can exist at its rim indefinitely, whatever happened to the satellites. I don't think you'll lose the ship, even though the core of the Singularity has the most bizarre architecture of any object in the Galaxy."

A metallic voice asked Buchanan if he wanted the approximation to continue. He waved a hand and it was silent. Buchanan waited.

"I talked to Mrs. Blankfort," said Kochan abruptly.

"And?" Buchanan said, throat dry.

"I share her views."

Buchanan held down the expostulations, the denials that sprang to his lips. He was prepared to lie with a steady determination.

Nothing would stand in his way, not now.

"Mrs. Blankfort's views?" he said mildly, a smile in place. "What are those, sir?"

Kochan fixed him with eyes like flat black stones.

"Any competent deep-space man who knew field theory could handle the assignment. Most would succeed in getting the required readings. You're too anxious for the job, Buchanan. You *need* to go to the Jansky Singularity."

"I told the Committee I thought I had a duty—"

"And so have I!" Kochan interrupted. Buchanan was startled by the iron in his voice. The man was used to command. He remembered vague stories of Kochan's enterprises: he had been ruthless in the pursuit of power. And then he had abandoned his career.

"I don't follow, Mr. Kochan."

"Buchanan, you owe me something."

"I owe you—"

"Your appointment."

"I'm grateful—'

"And more!"

"More?"

"Yes! You owe me what you've wanted for three years! The chance of revisiting the *Altair Star*."

Buchanan was stunned into silence.

Denial was useless. Kochan *knew*! The old woman had known. Yet she had been prepared to let events take their course. And now Kochan knew—he had conferred with the old psychologist who said she specialized in decision-making procedures. Buchanan sensed a mystery.

He said, calmly enough, though he could feel his heart hammering wildly: "The *Altair Star* can't be reached, sir."

Kochan's gaze dropped. The black eyes lost their hardness.

"The station is the only civilian ship which can be taken over by a human commander," said Kochan. "Getting the Committee to accept an overrider was difficult. Getting you as its commander was more of a problem. You'd not have got the assignment if I hadn't suppressed some reports," he said.

Buchanan gaped. Kochan could not be lying. He had an aura of complete sincerity, overwhelming certitude. But a member of the Committee deliberately falsifying information by suppressing reports!

"Mrs. Blankfort—" Buchanan began.

Kochan nodded.

"She guessed, but I prevailed on her. I think she understood my motives."

Buchanan's mind ranged frantically over what little he knew of Kochan's vast enterpreneurial activities. The man had exploited whole stellar colonies. His personal wealth was immense. He could have headed the Galactic Council. Was there some source of personal power in the Singularity? A mystery that he could turn to advantage? Some inconceivable way of using the energies of that bizarre space-time event?

Kochan produced a wallet.

"Look," he said, raw iron defeat on his face.

Buchanan saw the picture of a young woman in the first flush of adult beauty. Blonde hair cascaded to her shoulders. There was a confident smile, wide blue eyes, a slim neck and a firm bosom: she was intelligent, courageous, beautiful. Life lay before her and she wanted its fullness. He grabbed the wallet and stared.

"My only grandchild," said Kochan.

Buchanan understood, or half understood.

"She was—" He had seen her before.

"Yes."

Those wide blue eyes had looked out at him in slow-dawning comprehension; an infinite sadness had begun to swim into their depths. Buchanan knew her well, too well. It was the girl who had flirted with young Preston.

Buchanan wiped cold sweat from his forehead.

"If there had been anything I could have done," he said helplessly. "Anything!"

Kochan's black eyes were impassive again. He put the wallet away.

"I know, Buchanan."

Both men were lost for long seconds in despairing memories. Buchanan recovered first.

"I have to tell you, sir," he said, sick at heart. "There can be no chance—none! Not in a starquake like that!"

"I know she can't be brought back to life," said Kochan in his iron tones. "I know and accept it!"

"And you still want me to go to the *Altair Star*?"

There was no need for deception now.

"Yes."

"Why?"

Kochan's face was pinched, wizened, gnarled. Buchanan knew that worse monsters trod through his brain than those that afflicted his own tormented dreams.

"You simulated the interior of the Singularity just then," he grated. "But it's only a simulation—a projection! We don't know really what goes on at the middle of the accursed Singularity!"

"No, sir."

"Don't you see, Buchanan, that what terrifies me is not that my granddaughter is dead—"

Buchanan knew he was poised on the edge of a frightful knowledge.

"Sir?" he said, anxious for Kochan to continue, desperately afraid of the answer.

"I've checked on every known theory—all the variations of every conceivable hypothesis, every interpretation of all known readings! My God, Buchanan, I've devoted three years and enough wealth on research to build a fleet of *Altair Stars! And no one can prove that my granddaughter is at rest!*"

"But life can't continue without life-support systems, Mr. Kochan! The ship was half-wrecked! There wouldn't be air—energy—heat to sustain life for three years! Accept it," said Buchanan, afraid now. "She *must* be dead!"

Kochan fixed him with his black stonelike eyes.

"Buchanan, *I* was behind the building of the Singularity Station. I gave up all thoughts of personal ambition so that I could control the policies of the Committee. Only the Committee has the power to promote investigations of the Jansky Singularity, you see."

"Yes, sir."

The man's grim dedication and resolve matched his own. But what impelled him?

Buchanan heard, almost unbelieving, as Kochan went on:

"At the center of the Singularity is a core. And that core has properties that are not understood. Buchanan, believe me when I say this, that I have the best available evidence. There is a possibility that within the Singularity there is a kind of life that we cannot yet understand!"

"Life?"

"Human life—or inhuman life!"

"You think the people aboard the ship may be *alive*?"

"I want to know about my granddaughter!" Kochan was pleading with him. The old man went on: "All the theories I've been able to gather have been fed into the comps in your ship. When the time comes, listen to them. And then do what you have to do."

"You believe she may not be—*dead*?"

Buchanan did not want to ask his next question. It trespassed on an old man's innermost and most deeply-felt emotions. But he had to ask.

"You want me to find out?"

"Buchanan, there may be more than one way of dying. Make sure she is at rest!"

Stunned, Buchanan watched Kochan leave. He stood for several minutes staring at a blank, blue-pulsing screen without realizing it. He was brought back to a realization of the present by the slight oscillation of the ship as more of its systems were given their final tests.

There was much to think about.

But, meanwhile, there was work to do.

The small shuttle lifted off between the great infra-galactic ship's robot tugs, a minnow among salmon. The whine of engines thrusting out through the thin rain and then higher, past fifty-mile-high noctilucent clouds, came to Liz Deffant as an echo of her own silent howl of pain and loss. Within minutes, the shuttle would slide into the maw of the Enforcement Service vessel, and she would be cut off forever from the bitter, haunted man she wanted—needed!—and had lost to the ghosts of the past.

"Scan for the new Jansky Singularity Station," she ordered, surprising herself.

"Yes, Miss Deffant," an unseen automaton answered.

Before her a screen pulsed into life and the docking area swam into view. She reached forward and allowed a pair of clinging sensor-pads to latch onto the palms of her hand; their touch was unpleasant. *Closer*, she ordered, manipulating the pads with easy skill.

She saw figures moving about the black bulk of the ungainly vessel. A group of engineers were busy at one massive engine-pad.

Where was Al?

She saw a stooping, thin figure emerge tiredly. An old man. Who was he? She scanned closer still and saw a face she knew from many newscasts. Kochan. What was he doing there?

And still no sign of Al.

She almost ordered the scanners to cease probing, but she told herself she was entitled to one last look at Buchanan.

For over ten minutes she kept the scanners hunting for a sight of the lean, hard man she loved. And all the time she could feel the interest of the automatons which controlled the shuttle and obeyed her orders; already they would be reporting her interest in the almost-completed station. One more piece of information for the endless banks of comps far below the surface.

"Al!" she whispered as at last she saw the familiar honed features, the long sinewy frame, the bitter mouth which had begun to be able to ease into a smile.

There was a new expression on his face.

Before, he had looked tired, despairing, a man who thought of himself as a failure.

Now, he seemed completely lost. Cold, alone, lost.

She watched until the image shivered and began to fill with shadows. The great engines of the *ES 110* impinged on the little shuttle's own force-bands.

With a gentle shudder, the unmanned shuttle dropped into the dock of the looming infragalactic ship.

CHAPTER 4

Eleven members of the Board for the Regulation of Space Hazards turned out for the launching of the Jansky Singularity Station. There was a minimum of coverage by the news media. Buchanan's appointment had stirred the newscasters to a fresh appraisal of the dangers of the Jansky Singularity, and they emphasized especially the loss of the *Altair Star*; but interest soon waned. Kochan had used some of his vast, submerged powers to see that the affair was played down. Yet nothing of the turmoil that surged in Kochan's mind was reflected on his face as he shook Buchanan's hand and wished him a successful voyage and a safe return.

It was a cold day, with a chill wind howling among the docked ships. Buchanan saw that Mrs. Blankfort was ill, and worried too. There was an anxious look in her deep-sunken eyes. He knew that her concern was for him. The members of the Board withdrew to take warm drinks when the brief ceremony of commissioning was over.

Buchanan entered the ship and forgot them.

And then he waited as an enormous tug latched onto the squat ugly station.

"Jansky Station clear for lift-off," a metallic voice told him. "Engaging first stage of flight schedule."

"Yes," said Buchanan, hardly able to believe that the days had passed and that now the ship trembled around him as the tug exerted its huge powers.

"Second stage commencing now," the robot told him.

"Good."

There was nothing to be said, nothing to be done, for the station and its throw-away monstrous tug were in robotic hands until they reached the edges of the colossal rotating enigma that had clawed in so many unwary ships. Then the tug would fall away. And the station would be his.

"You should take your position for lift-off," the robot voice told him.

Buchanan looked at the cone-shaped pedestal which was the station's robot overseer. Anger shook him momentarily. Mrs. Blankfort was wrong. You could hate the robots. Even if they were capable of making far better decisions than any human mind in the uncertain reaches between the spiraling arms of the Galaxy.

The ship was poised now, almost a living thing.

Buchanan settled into the soft couch. Tendrils of resilient plastics settled in a web around him. Power raged into the main drive of the tug. The edges of the large deck began to blur as the ship began to enter into the disagreeable phenomenon of Phase. Sharp angles became rounded, straight lines took on uneasy curves, flat surfaces bent and rose up eerily.

"Lift-off, Commander Buchanan?"

It was a formality, a concession to the lost status of the nominal commander. An ironical request, part of an old ritual. The robot was programmed to ask his permission to begin the long voyage.

"Proceed," said Buchanan formally.

"Welcome aboard, Miss Deffant," the commander of the *ES 110* said to Liz Deffant. She appreciated the frank sincerity of his admiration. "You're not exactly what we expected, you know. We got the authorization for a New Settlements Bureau ecologist, female, and they usually turn out to be large and dedicated and not altogether—well, *feminine*." He paused and took in the sharp thrust of the well-formed breasts and the promise of the firm long legs. "Not what we expected at all."

Liz smiled at him. It took no effort at all. He was a youngish man, not yet thirty, short and broad, with heavy features and hair like wire. When he grinned he showed large white teeth, and his eyes shone with pleasure. She wondered if it was a sign of recovery that she could respond to his animal good spirits.

"This isn't what I expected of an Enforcement Service ship," she said. It wasn't.

There was nothing to distinguish the control deck of the big infragalactic ship from, say, one of the New Settlements Bureau's larger support ships, the kind that had acted as a back-up station when she was working the Ophiuchi Complex. There were operations screens, the usual robotic control pedestal, the banks of consoles with weaving sensor-pads alert to fasten onto a human palm, the big command chair for the human commander—the usual setup; and an unexpected spaciousness. She had expected more spartan conditions, perhaps a feeling of oppressive detention.

"Tell me what you expected, Miss Deffant."

"Liz."

"I'm Jack Rosario. You'll meet the others when we eat."

"The crew?"

"We carry six, including myself." Rosario's gesture took in the controls. "So tell me what you expected."

Liz looked about the bright bridge, all golden yellow and green plastics. "It doesn't look like a traveling jail. I could be on a tourist deck—I thought you'd all be carrying side arms—"

"Side arms!" hooted Rosario. "Phasers!"

"Well—"

"No! There's no need. Not since we went fully automatic. We haven't gone in for that sort of thing since the coma-cells were introduced."

"Coma-cells?"

"We've used them for years. Its easier for all of us—crew, guards, expellees. We're entirely automatic."

"You put the expellees into a coma?"

"Yes. Haven't you seen an Enforcement Service ship before?"

"I've *seen* them. Twice. But I've never been aboard one so far. Not until now. It wasn't my idea. It's just that I wanted to get back to Messier 16 as soon as I could."

Rosario's broad face was interested, but he did not follow up with a question; he caught the hint of regret in her voice. She liked the way he did not pursue the subject.

"So we should be wearing side arms and have bunches of keys on our belts. And you should hear chains rattling and prisoners groaning." He grinned. "And there'd be water and a bone you wouldn't care to identify. That it?"

Liz smiled again. Rosario was like the people she remembered from her home planet. Straightforward, kindly, competent. Not bitter and lost. Not at all like Al.

"I was wrong."

Rosario looked at her speculatively.

"You're with Galactic Service. You must be well thought of to get a shuttle out to us. Would it disturb you too much to see how we carry the prisoners?"

Liz felt, for the first time, the authoritative strength of Jack Rosario. He was a member of a service which carried out with a ruthless efficiency the judgments and penalties of the Galactic courts. Enforcement meant just that. Find offenders, bring them to the courts, and ferry those expelled out to the Rim. Rosario was the commander of an expellee-transport. He was offering to show her the human cargo of the *ES 110*: the prisoners.

"I don't know," said Liz honestly.

"Think about it."

He called a low-grade robot servitor to show her to a guest cabin. She noticed that the robot was constructed along heavier lines than the usual run of servitors. Its antennas scanned her, and she was sure that a complete rundown of her physical characteristics was already on its way to the Enforcement Service vessel's memory-banks. There was a hint of menace in its squat, armored bulk.

She wondered if she had made a mistake.

A few more days at Center would have been tolerable.

Buchanan waited until the mad corybantics of warped force-bands settled to a comprehensible pattern as the tug drilled through the continuums on its vast, looping voyage toward the bizarre Singularity. It seemed that small metallic hands clawed at the fabric of his brain, such was the shock of the first moments of thrust. The station had not the stability of an infragalactic liner. It was small. A small blip containing the life-support systems for one man, but a blip that would soon ride on three enormous storehouses of energy. The sheer brute power was needed if the ship was to hold in the unreal dimensions.

Buchanan gloated in the latent power of those three great pods. Strange configurations existed within the Singularity. Ordinary ships would be swamped by one blind spasm. The station was built to withstand the unknown.

Would it?

When the ship was riding more easily, Buchanan pushed aside the clinging limpet-like tendrils that held him. He stood up and shook his head. Black light flashed before his eyes, but the worst was over.

"Give me an estimate of the duration of the voyage," he ordered the robot controller.

"We're holding onto a subgalactic surge," said the robotic controller. "It's a large wave, sir. Present estimates put the ship's arrival at the Singularity in seventeen hours, sir. That is, of course, approximately. It could be a little less."

"It could?" Buchanan said, without interest. At one time he would have checked the projections for the weird path among the starways of the continuums. It would have pleased him to see what interstellar gales they could have ridden among, what freak quakings of expiring supernovas they could have caught onto to add impetus to the great surge of the engines. Not now. Let the robots do the easy work. The routine duties.

"What's happening at the Singularity?"

"No measurable changes since the last batch of reports, sir. It maintains a regular rotating shape, giving the readings of a gaseous fluid bound by its own gravitational attraction. No profound seismological disturbances of the kind associated with starquake, sir."

It was reassuring. No sign yet of the monstrous Singularity ripping space apart. No starquake. The thing within the Singularity could set up a time-space event that shattered the continuums around it with a colossal flurry of unknown forces. And if a ship should chance to be nearby, then that ship was lost. But now the Singularity was quiescent.

At the moment it was a bland, eerie, alien beast: an event in the Galaxy like no other. An inexplicable thing, unguessable, alone, singular, as the old-time physicists had it, a *Singularity*! At present, inactive.

"A drink," said Buchanan.

"Yes, sir."

Ice tinkled in the glass. Buchanan followed the single drink with a request for a modest meal. "I'll eat," he said.

It was forthcoming within two minutes.

Buchanan looked at the well-done steak and the salad. Then at the glass of wine, deep-red, full-bodied, delicious. He smiled. An endless recycling. All of it back through his own system into the tanks, then out to the culture-frames, then to the preparation-units; and so onto a silver tray brought by a deferential servitor. There was an excellent catering service. The Board had gone to some trouble to provide for his particular tastes. He laughed.

This meal could be the last of its kind.

He savored it, just as he savored the memory of the girl with the golden-brown eyes who had reached in pity to wipe the deep lines from his forehead. It had been such a near thing too. He had almost returned to a normal life, almost cast off the load of guilt and grief that rode him like some great foul wen.

Another man, much older, took over the bridge when Rosario said it was time to eat. He was introduced as Poole. Liz had the feeling he resented her presence aboard the *ES 110*. She understood, she thought. Few women would serve on such ships. It was one area of public service which was almost entirely a male preserve.

The crew she met at dinner were equally impressed by Liz Deffant. Two were Security men, another, like Jack Rosario, a crewman. They were introduced one by one.

Liz remembered their names carefully. The Security men were large and alike in physical appearance: tough, hard-looking men in their thirties. There was a Dieter and a Mack. Rosario explained that a third was on duty. He ate later. A young fair-haired man who followed Liz's every movement with an unbelieving wide-eyed stare was called Tup.

The conversation was general, mostly questions about Liz's experiences with the New Settlements Bureau. She told them about the last project she had worked on, the experiments with Terran-type plant-life on a fairly hostile planet in the Ophiuchi Complex. It had absorbed her, and the men recognized that she spoke with knowledge and enthusiasm. They had enough technical knowledge to grasp the central problem—the planet had an aberrant gravitational core, so plants didn't grow with the same kind of cell-structure as on Terran-type worlds; rejigging the planet's heavy metal core was possible, but that involved the possibility of disturbing several other ecological features. The Bureau regarded major reconstruction as a last resort.

She explained how they had been baffled until someone came up with the idea of making a slight molecular realignment of new root formation to give the newly-introduced plants a firmer base; and that had done the trick. When she finished she realized that she had not thought of Buchanan for an hour. It seemed like a betrayal. She could not be glad about it. She was silent for minutes.

Rosario worried, Liz could see. He stared at her when he thought she was not watching him, and he frowned when the meal was over. The others left, except for Tup. Liz was aware that they sensed her misery.

"Does it worry you—the fact that we are a transport for expellees?" asked Rosario.

"No," said Liz. It did, though. Subtly, there was a sense of tired and defeated evil aboard the Enforcement Service vessel.

"Would you like to see the cells?" said Tup eagerly.

"You could," agreed Rosario. They were both making a strong effort to please her; but Liz had no special desire to see the condemned men and women.

"I don't think so."

"You're not against the idea of transporting the expellees out to the Rim, are you, Liz?" asked Rosario. "Is that what's troubling you?"

"I don't think so," said Liz, hesitantly. "But don't worry about me. I'm sorry if I seem to be out of sorts—please don't worry about me."

Rosario grinned.

"All right. Now I have to go to the bridge. It's Poole's turn to eat." To Tup he said, "If you can get Miss Deffant to change her mind, show her around the ship."

The youth could hardly believe his luck. "Me, Jack—sir?"

"She's with Galactic," said Rosario. "No restrictions." As he was walking across to the grav-chute, Tup said; "Miss Deffant could have a look at Maran."

"Maran!" Liz was shocked into the exclamation.

Rosario stopped. He saw Liz's distress, yet his face was hard.

It could have been the wild and bitter days of the Mad Wars all over again. Maran was the greatest cyberneticist of all time. The human mind: that was his workshop. Maran's obsession was the inner depths. Liz shivered. She knew something of obsessions. In a small way, Buchanan was an example of what utter obsessiveness could do. Maran was the far extreme.

"When I think what he did—" she began.

"And what he hoped to do," Rosario said.

"Come and see him," said Tup, who looked from Liz to the *ES 110*'s commander. "You'll never get the chance again."

"No," said Rosario. "No one will. Except those at the Rim."

She knew what he meant. A humane Galaxy had reverted to the oldest law of all. Those who could not live by a community's code of ethics must leave. When there was no possibility of redemption, when a man or woman put himself or herself beyond any hope of forgiveness, the verdict was inevitable. To do more was barbarous. To do less was to imperil the community.

The aberrant were cast out.

"There's nothing to be alarmed about, Miss Deffant," said Tup. He was, perhaps, enjoying her discomfiture. "Maran's unconscious. They all are. Coming, Miss Deffant?"

Maran aboard the ship. Liz did not answer for some seconds. She was still absorbing the idea that he was somewhere in the cavernous depths of the prison-ship.

I can open a million years of evolution, was his simple, sublime claim. *If a few must be sacrificed to show what the human mind is, then why not?*

Liz caught herself gasping at the simple enormity of what he said. And at the center of it all, a terrifying logic.

"Don't press her," ordered Rosario.

"You won't get the chance again, Miss Deffant," Tup insisted. He grinned placatingly at Rosario. "She can tell them at Messier 16 that she saw Maran."

"Don't go down if you don't want to," Rosario said.

Liz's thoughts were confused. She had seen the news-casts, with Maran stating his case so lucidly. There was a calmness about him that had fascinated all who saw him. And Maran was absolutely right in his main point.

Man was a unique phenomenon. There was only one intelligence in the whole of the Galaxy. Perhaps in the whole of creation. *It must be understood, this thing called man*, Maran had said. *We must know the when and the how and the why of its beginnings!*

When the gruesome details of Maran's experiments were revealed, it was difficult to equate the calmness with the horrific things he had done to follow human beings. *We must gouge out the secrets of a million years*, he had insisted. *Find the beginning, understand the mechanism of transition from thing to man!*

There was only one mystery, according to Maran. The mind of man. And he had devised his strange machines to investigate the human psyche. At first there were volunteers. The Enforcement Service moved in when the news of what had happened to them began to filter out. By that time, he had agents recruiting "helpers" in remote and primitive systems. Gullible men and women responded to his promises of wealth and mystical power. They were furious when the cruisers shipped them back to their barbaric planets. Maran had charisma. His simple, monumental message had enormous potency.

Find the moment of man's emergence to knowledge! Hold the moment, freeze it in time: examine, understand, develop it: and build the psyche into a cosmic engine! Liz recalled the arguments. To so many, they had become a catechism.

"Suppose he's right," she found herself saying to the two Enforcement Service crewmen.

"Maran right?" Rosario asked.

"Yes!"

"How, Miss Deffant? How right?" Tup wanted to know.

She could hardly put it into words, but she knew what she wanted to convey. Maran had pointed out that, despite all the attempts to communicate with supposed alien intelligences in other island universes, there had been no answers. Vast scanners ranged the depths of the Universe. They had sensed no coherent emissions. Despite the huge beamers which tried to tell far galaxies of the existence of the human race there had been no response. Couldn't it be, Liz asked herself, that man was entirely alone in the Universe? Maran said so.

She collected her thoughts.

"I meant, what if he's right about our being the only advanced life-form?" Before they could answer, she went on: "Oh, I know there have been theories about intelligent minerals operating on a time-scale too slow for us to understand—I even went for the notion of intelligent stars when they found that crazy double-star, but not now—you see, I've been *around*! I've been to all kinds of planets—I've seen insect-eating lichens, walking plants, fossils that wake up once every millennium and then go back to sleep—but I've never come across anything that I can *talk* to! Nothing! And neither has anyone else!"

Tup was startled by the flow of words, but Rosario was not. New Settlements people had this enthusiasm. It came from their planetfalls on strange worlds which might soon echo to the building of towns. They had to be dreamers.

Liz realized that Rosario was waiting for her to go on. She saw his strong square face and looked at him for the first time as she would look at any handsome man. A stray recollection came back. Buchanan. Al Buchanan. He had looked so helpless the first time she had seen him. Not weak, but hurt. Not at all determined, like Rosario. But Al and Rosario were of a type. There was strength in the Enforcement Service commander's steady gaze: he would make up his mind and act. Perhaps not as obsessively as Al. Other memories clamored for attention as she tried to marshal her inchoate arguments. Liz recalled small, intense private pleasures from the first days with Buchanan. A tiny victory when he said he would not run the recordings of the Court of Inquiry anymore. The feeling of dried leaves kicked up by their feet as they plowed through an autumn wood. The day they decided to freelance. There had been so many good days.

"Maran, Miss Deffant?" prompted Tup, who had not developed Rosario's patience.

She realized that they were politely waiting for her to make up her mind. The decision, and the answer, came:

"I'll see him. Not because I want to tell anyone I've seen him. It's just that I wonder about the man who thinks—believes—we're unique."

"Take Miss Deffant," said Rosario. He smiled at Liz. "I think Maran could be right too."

"Jack?" said Tup, in surprise. "*You* think he's right?"

"Yes. Right about the uniqueness of the human mind. Maybe we are the only advanced form of life in the whole of the Universe. Maybe we should find out what caused this thing we call intellect or intelligence or soul."

Liz hesitated. "You think Maran was right to try to solve the mystery—of how we started?"

"He was in too much of a hurry. If he's right, if there is some way of understanding the processes of human thought and building on them, then we needn't hurry. We've been around a long time. There's no need to force the pace."

"This way, Miss Deffant," Tup said. He could not help adding: "This way to the Chamber of Horrors!"

There was the usual grav-chute. At the bottom, Tup announced their arrival to an unseen robot servitor. "I'm bringing a female visitor with full Security clearance," he told it. To Liz he added: "Regulations. We have to comply."

A shield slid away and Liz saw the cell-deck.

A Security guard came across, to be introduced as Pete. Liz waved to him, but she barely noticed his polite smile, nor his brief welcoming words. She was spellbound, rooted to the spot, dazed by the sight of the unconscious expellees in the eerie green subdued lights of the enormous hold.

It was so much bigger than she expected. And nothing had prepared Liz for the shock of seeing rows of tanks, each with its gently swaying body cushioned by a grayish ooze. Tup had spoken of a Chamber of Horrors. It was. The unconscious figures were subtly sinister, like so many effigies of once-fearsome men and women. Liz tried to control her shaking hands. She felt fear, sensed it deep within her body.

"They don't feel a thing!" declared Tup.

Wrapped up in her own reaction as she was, Liz could recognize a change in the young man's tone. He too sense the chilled malice that emanated from the scores of tanks.

A green iridescence picked out the features of the expellees. Young, old, some women but mostly men. Near-naked bodies bobbed in a pulsating ooze. All the minds blotted out, monitored by machines below the tanks. There was no rational cause for fear, thought Liz. But she felt fear. It was not the corpselike appearance of the expellees, nor the eerie glow of the subdued lighting, nor yet the soft squelching of the ooze as bodies slipped and slid about the tanks; none of these things mattered, for she knew that they were held in a state of unconsciousness deep below the normal level of sleep. The cause of her fear was other than these.

Tup laughed. It was a young man's reaction, thoughtless and without malice. "There's nothing to worry about!" he added at once. "They can't harm you!"

She knew it. Yet there was a sense of ragged, contained violence in the cell-deck. She shuddered, conscious of the empty stares of the unconscious expellees.

"It's their eyes," said Liz.

Pete nodded. "It's something you have to get used to."

All three looked into the nearest coma-cell where a large and powerfully-built yet flabby man lay. His eyes seemed to transfix them with a straining, questioning intensity.

Liz shuddered again. Empty eyes, glaring into the emptiness of empty dreams.

"Is that him?' She knew she spoke as if the man in the tank could hear.

There was a hostile quality in Tup's voice when he replied: "That's Maran."

CHAPTER 5

The Singularity was near.

Already the vague emanations from its strange depths were impinging upon the sensitive scanners of the station. On the operations screen, which occupied almost the whole of one side of the bridge, an image of the coordinates of the Singularity was forming. Pulsing with a vicious energy, the bizarre space-time event announced its presence. Trails of discontinuous energy fields scored the region inhabited by the Singularity. It was a leprous patch on the screen, a corroding and waiting beast poised, grim, blind.

Buchanan knew the configuration of the Singularity. Its unquestioned dangers he admitted; but they held no terrors for him. Soon, the robots would loose the tug and when it fell away he would point the station directly into the maw of the Singularity. But now he had other considerations.

Kochan had spoken in terms that had urged new fears into his mind. The passengers and crew of the *Altair Star* were lost—dead, irretrievably gone, lost. Buchanan's self-appointed task was to find why the robots had given up so easily; *why* they had announced that no action on their part—or on the part of any human, by implication, since they regarded themselves as far superior to humans—could possibly do anything to save the huge liner. And that task had seemed enough. To find the reason for the loss of his ship. But now there was more. Kochan had loosed fresh devils to haunt him.

Was it possible that, within the vast, rotating phenomenon, the victims of the tragedy were held in a fantastic chronoclasm?

Buchanan fed instructions to the sensor-pads in his palms. The screen cleared, pulsed with dim light, and then projected a fresh image. Buchanan stared for minutes, watching the ship's progress.

The ship—the station—coasted easily along the inner arm of a spiraling vortex that helped flip it, like some cosmic slingshot, toward the dark regions: always with economy and efficiency toward the Singularity. The ship was being handled superbly. He admitted it. He had hours now, hours in which to think over Kochan's new and frightening ideas.

He approached the robotic controller and spoke to the cone-shaped pedestal: "The Singularity," he said.

"Sir?" grated a metallic voice.

"Mr. Kochan left information. Give it. Begin."

"Yes, sir."

Buchanan watched. With growing dismay, he saw graphs, readings, projections: the foundation of Kochan's fears. It *was* possible.

"That's Maran," agreed the guard.

The three of them looked at the lax body. A slow surge within the tank brought the bulk of the chest and belly higher. It was like the surfacing of some great creature from the lower depths. But for the eyes, it might have been a comic sight.

Liz shivered. Here was the source of the unease in the cell-deck.

"Miss, why don't you go and look at the rest of the ship?"

The Security guard indicated a wide grav-chute at the far end of the cavernous hold. At the same time a slight shake of his head alerted Tup to Liz's state of shock. Tup was perceptive.

"Not more like this!" Liz shuddered.

"No!" Tup said at once. "Come on, Miss Deffant—you have to see the survival-pods. What's in them, how they're launched. You'll be interested—you've done some pioneering." He took her arm, for once unembarrassed. "It wasn't such a good idea bringing you down here. We'll go down to the deck below."

Liz allowed herself to be led past the rows of green-glowing tanks. She tried to avoid the empty stares of the expellees, but it was difficult. If she had been properly in control of herself and able to state her inclination, she would have asked to be returned to her cabin. But the slightly dazed and considerably fearful state of mind that troubled her made her suggestible. She followed Tup to a grav-chute at the far end of the cell-deck and again found herself floating downward to the further recesses of the great infragalactic vessel.

Tup rattled on cheerfully about the method of propelling the prisoners once they reached the far star at the Rim. Small, individual craft took the awakening expellees to their new lives.

"Here they are!" Tup announced.

She was in a huge cargo hold. But this deck was bright and cheerful. No lines of tanks, no eerie half-lights, nothing one could easily associate with the Enforcement Service. The hold was full, however.

Liz saw scores of tall white cylinders, each one about twice the height of a man. Their purpose was obvious.

"The survival pods," said Tup. He pointed to a small lock. "That's where we launch them—all automatically. The expellees are shunted down here by the robot servitors, then they're taken through a fairly slow revivifying process. When they wake up, they're in a glide path."

Liz inspected one of the cylinders. She made out the small propulsion unit.

"We carried individual life rafts something like them, but not so small as these."

"They're not designed for deep-space use—though they would last for about six hours. We launch the expellees at predetermined coordinates that give them a flight of only a few minutes. Want to see inside one?"

Liz shook her head. She was still shivering, though the temperature in the hold was tolerable, comfortable even.

Tup was disappointed. "Doubt if you'll get the chance again," he offered. "It's bending regulations to open them, but you'd be interested." He grinned, shy once more as he realized they were alone. "I had Pete program you on the console as a crew-member. Coming?"

"All right," said Liz. She examined the gleaming canister without seeing it properly. There were instructions. The words did not reach her mind. There was something troubling her, but she could not quite say what. And if she had been able to identify it, she knew she would not want to speak of it. Something about the eyes . . .

"Look—everything they need for survival!" announced Tup as he opened one of the pods. "We launch them just outside the gaseous envelope—they glide down in a preset path. By the time he lands, the expellee is fully awakened. Ready to start again."

Liz shook her head and concentrated dutifully; she studied the contents of the capsule with a professional eye. Tup was right. It was a neatly-designed survival pack. The expellees would not starve. The doubts and fears she had felt were pushed to the back of her mind. She checked the contents.

"Water purification plant, seasonal calculator, tools, medical outfit."

"Simple expansion-principle weapon in unassembled form," supplemented Tup. "Where they're going they could run across carnivores."

Liz glanced at the package. She was uninterested in weaponry, however primitive or quaint.

"Location of chief mineral deposits; water cycle. It's a full ecological rundown," Liz said. "It's comprehensive. They'll not starve."

"I've thought of trying one of the pods out," agreed Tup. "You know—take a vacation and live the simple life."

"They'll certainly be doing that," Liz said.

"After what they've done, they can't complain."

Liz heard the edge of iron in Tup's tone. He too was more than he seemed. A shy youth, there was resolution and authority beneath the bashful exterior.

"Well," said Liz, with an attempt at lightness, "with that kind of rudimentary equipment they won't be coming back."

Tup was not smiling when he replied. "That's the idea."

At the entrance to the shaft that would take them up to the deck above and its grim lines of half-lit tanks, Liz hesitated. On impulse she said:

"Would you think it foolish if I said something about the cell-deck?"

"No."

"It was the prisoner, Maran."

"Jano Maran," said Tup, not at all boyishly. "He worried you?"

"It was something I thought I saw."

"Saw? Maran?"

"It was the eyes!"

Tup nodded. "It's hard to think that they're in a deep hypno-sleep."

Liz hesitated, feeling foolish now. But she went on with a rush: "He was watching! I'm sure he was!"

Tup smiled. "Their central nervous systems are keyed into the comps. Breathing—food intake—waste products—every metabolic system is monitored. They're held in a complex state deep below normal sleep. Getting them out of it is a long and tricky process. Each expellee has his own program for a return to consciousness. They just *can't* do it on their own. Any premature awakening could be dangerous, possibly fatal. They'll be kept under until some hours before they reach the planet we've taken over from your Bureau. Out at the Rim. Miss Deffant, Maran wasn't watching you. It really is impossible. Believe me?"

"Thanks," said Liz Deffant.

They passed the rows of bobbing figures, Liz staying close to the slight figure of the young man. He was enjoying her dependence on him.

"We have complete automatic control of the expellees," he went on, keeping to a neutral tone to show that he had no need especially to reassure her. "They feel nothing. It's hardly necessary to monitor them, but the machines do so. We're superfluous, really."

"I suppose so," said Liz Deffant. She was feeling better. The sense of oppression began to lift as they neared the next grav-chute. It would not be long before she transferred to the Messier 16 shuttle. She would not go to the cell-deck again, Liz decided.

"Ask Pete—Pete!"

The figure of the Security guard was in almost complete darkness, shadowed as he was by a bank of sensors. Tup went across, grinning.

"Aren't we just spare parts?" he was saying, but Liz did not hear.

Impelled by a compulsive curiosity, she had stopped at the tank containing the figure of the expellee Maran. It was morbid, she knew, but she wanted to make sure that she was wrong about the eyes. Those terrible eyes!

Liz looked down.

The eerie half-light played on a mottled face, a mouth wide-open, with the tongue thrusting out blackly . . . and the eyes. Wide-open in mute appeal, but dead. Blank and dead—not unseeing, *dead.*

And not Maran's eyes.

Liz screamed. She knew who lay in the tank. It was the Security guard Tup had called to.

She looked away, stepping backward in acute mind-reeling terror. Tup's contorted features glared back at her. She saw big hands at his neck, holding him in a frightful clasp.

Tup clawed once at the hands, and then something cracked with an abrupt, sickening finality. The hands relaxed. Tup slid toward Liz.

She knew who had killed him. The impossible had happened. It was the man from the tank: Jano Maran.

CHAPTER 6

Buchanan was oppressed by his solitude. He had not yet grown accustomed once more to his burden of guilt: a residual remnant of Liz Deffant's gentle, persistent, affectionate presence still lingered. *Forget her*, he told himself. *Finished. Over.*

He studied the information left by Kochan. That was his life now, all of it. There was no room for tenderness. He had to be as unfeeling as the automatons. *Cold. Logical. Inhuman.*

"I'll check the main features and you agree if I've got them right," he told the robot controller.

"Yes, Commander."

"First, the central core of the Singularity could be a superdense form of neutron star or star formation."

"Yes, sir."

"If that's so, it contains an area where the gravitational pull is a hundred billion times what would be normal on an Earth-type planet." It was inconceivable, so much pressure.

"About that, sir."

"The core is ultradense and stable, the crust brittle and fragile. When the crust breaks under gravitational strain the result is starquake."

"Yes, sir."

A tiny superdense core ground in on itself by those fantastic pressures. And then, cracking—*starquake*!

"And associated distortion of temporal field," Buchanan said slowly. "Chronoclasm. The disruption of time."

"It's only a theory, sir. The rest is reasonably well substantiated by automatic readings over fifty years. All recorded data associates the cracking of the crust with starquake. But discontinuous temporal alignments haven't been recorded."

"Mainly because we wouldn't know what to record them with," said Buchanan.

"Quite, sir."

"So it's a guess," said Buchanan, unable to accept the implications of what he had learned. "Time dislocation isn't proved."

"Agreed, sir. Mr. Kochan's team saw it as a strong hypothesis but only one of several. For instance, sir, it's predicted that the Singularity contains what's called a 'black hole'—an area that contracts to infinity. Again, sir, there may be a combination of such a black hole *and* a neutron star or star cluster. But Mr. Kochan dissented. He holds to the time-distortion elements with an illogical fervor."

Buchanan's gaze was grim. Kochan was obsessed by an idea which was peculiarly horrifying.

"Let's assume Mr. Kochan's right," he told the robot. "Assume time-bending or distortion could occur within the Singularity. What projections do you have, given this?"

"Two distinct possibilities, sir. Both unverifiable."

"How's that?"

"The station would have to enter the Singularity to get the necessary data, sir. And that isn't your assignment."

Buchanan bared his teeth in a humorless grin. The robot would soon be disillusioned as to the station's mission.

"The two possibilities," he said.

"Yes, sir. One is that there are slight distortions locally which would give a well-known effect—a slight disjunction of the time-scale between events inside and outside the Singularity with a difference measurable in microseconds. There are certain parallels in collapsing supernova readings."

Wrong, thought Buchanan. Nothing in the experience of man in his exploration of the Galaxy would be like the interior of the uncertain regions. Whatever forces boiled up during and after a supernova, they did not begin to match the weird qualities of the Singularity's emissions. A difference of microseconds!

"The other?"

It was the theory he had projected once Kochan's information began to flow. He had already formed a strong opinion, but he wanted the machines to confirm his interpretation. The fearful one. The interpretation which Kochan dreaded.

"A severe dislocation of temporal patterns."

"How severe?"

"Time would stop."

"Stop! *Stop*?"

Buchanan had not gone that far. Time bent. Time flowing sidereally. Time utterly out of joint. But time *stopped*!

The robot waited for a minute and went on: "A most extreme possibility, sir."

"I hope so," said Buchanan.

He thought of the *Altair Star* lapsing into the strange dimensions, falling away and into that gaping black maw . . . all those lives. Into what?

"And what of the effect on the *Altair Star*?" he demanded harshly. "On the humans aboard?"

The robot showed him an image of force-bands held in a bizarre equilibrium. Time hung still.

"If the theory holds good, sir, then there would be a state of suspended animation."

Buchanan saw that this too was possible.

"But they died! They all died!"

"Clinical death is not easy to establish, sir," the robot pointed out. "In humans the precedent is the cessation of all forms of electrical activity in the nervous system."

"Well?"

"For all electrical activity to cease, there has to be an outlet for the energy, sir. It must be dissipated somehow."

Buchanan had a vision of frozen, undead, undying men and women, of children poised for the final moment.

"They couldn't live for three years!" snarled Buchanan, conscious of the pointlessness of his rage.

"There should be the condition known as 'death,'" agreed the calm untroubled metallic voice.

"And there may not be!" grated Buchanan.

"Pushing the theory to a conclusion, sir, it may be said that the passengers and crew of the *Altair Star* might not have had enough time to die."

Buchanan experienced a lurching sense of horror. The robot had given the inevitable confirmation. Had he sensed, in the haunted eyes of the fair haired girl, that already she was aware of a shadowy kind of existence beyond time and death?

"It couldn't be," Buchanan said, believing that it could.

"We are talking only of theory, sir," the robot voice said calmly into the aseptic, quietly-humming emptiness of the bridge.

And what a theory, thought Buchanan. More than ever, he was sure he had been right to seize the opportunity presented by the building of the Jansky Station. Right, too, to give up even a Liz Deffant.

"Only a theory," he repeated. "I hope so."

The unreasoning terror held Liz for minutes. During this time, she could neither think nor move. Etched on her mind was the sight of the young Enforcement Service crewman's death. Tup. She did not know his full name. And now he was dead.

The general circumstances of the scene impinged on her mind, but not with any coherent force. She could see pain and bewilderment on Maran's ooze-flecked face. Dimly she was aware that he was suffering. She could see that he was moving with slow, hesitant steps, about the area of the console. She knew too that he had seen her—and disregarded her. But the shock of Tup's death prevented her from being able to analyze or react.

She could not even scream.

Tup had been laughing. He had approached the figure of the guard and surprised the expellee Maran. Maran had turned, reached. . . .

Her eyes were fixed, staring. They were almost unfocused. She tried to scream. Nothing came. She recognized that Maran looked at her again.

In the two or three minutes of her total immobility, he halted the local command structure of the cell-deck. He subverted the robots. Liz could see, hear, watch with some kind of awareness, but she could do nothing. Maran ignored her.

"This system advises all human crew and Security guards to remain calm," announced a metallic voice from the console. "Servitors will investigate emergency on cell-deck."

Maran heard and moved. There was an hierarchical structure of robotic control in the big ship. Systems controlled groups of lesser systems. At the moment, the Grade Two system which administered the cell-deck was dealing with a situation it recognized.

"Emergency on cell-deck!" reported another, more authoritative voice. It was almost human. "Emergency procedure five-eight-stroke-two will be carried out."

"Agreed!" the cell-deck supervisor answered. "Low-grade servitors will apprehend released expellee forthwith.

Malfunctioning of metabolic monitors will be investigated!"

Deep within the vessel, tiny crablike maintenance machines began to skitter toward the dusty service passages.

In Maran's slow-clearing mind there was an image of the robot's instant response to the information that a prisoner had been freed. He looked at his big hands, briefly checked that the girl was still in shock, and acted.

Liz was aware, somewhere at the fringes of her mind, that heavy, armored servitors were moving. The deck below her feet quivered. Two robots slid past her. Restraint tentacles flowed smoothly from their squat bodies. Maran was a dark blur at the console. His hands began to weave over the controls of the cell-deck as the robots faced him.

"Do not move!" ordered a raw, cold voice. "You are subject to restraint order under Galactic Council Penal Code Regulations."

"You are an expellee and must be returned to coma-cell," added the second servitor.

Liz Deffant slowly surfaced. It was over. Whatever calamitous accident had released Maran would be put right. The brief nightmare, the terror and the horror, were over. Liz could begin to feel a sense of relief. The robots must prevail against Maran. The guard had been taken unawares; Tup had died unknowing.

But the robots knew what they faced. The two low-grades moved like clever animals, one to each side of the console.

"Yes!" said Liz, a sharp satisfaction in her voice. "Get him!"

Maran was punching commands. A tentacle cautiously flicked out. A bronchitic metal-lined voice called:

"Human interference with command console is not permitted unless authorized by Grade One system! You are a human. You must move away. You are under restraint order!"

The second machine added its warning: "Move away at once otherwise restraint procedures will be used!"

Maran flinched—Liz could see the big body shake—at the touch of the hawser-like tentacle. He turned toward the dim lit cell-deck, with its rows of silent, gently-bobbing men and women. Liz could not help a sensation of vengeful satisfaction. Two lives cut off in minutes—the guard and Tup.

Maran slammed a huge hand down on the bank of controls.

The eerie cell-deck became a place of ghastly, convulsed terrifying confusion.

A scream of protest came from a dozen robotic throats. The flood of metallic howls, each one stepped up in volume to make itself heard above the others, blasted at Liz. Pain rocked her. She put her hands to her ears, the first move she had made since she saw Tup die. She was deafened by the uproar of the robots.

"Emergency!" screamed one robotic voice above the others. "Expellee restraint systems broken down! Malfunction in cell-deck—"

"Condition of restraint broken!" confirmed another, still louder. "This system has no data for release of expellees in condition phase!"

Even through her hands, Liz could make out the sense of the most clamorous reports. And she could see that the two servitors were affected by the massive confusion all around her. They had stopped, feet short of Maran. Black tentacles began to retract. Dull-gleaming carapaces looked about the cell-deck with almost a human bewilderment.

Maran's hands were busy at the controls.

What was he doing? Liz thought dazedly.

"Confused instruction!" the Grade Two robot complained. "Instructions for the release of expellees have been received contrary to standing orders! Confirmation from Grade One system requested!"

"This low-grade servitor is confused!" agreed the robot nearest Maran.

"This low-grade servitor also!" added its companion. "No further instructions have been received since release of all expellees was ordered. Does this instruction supercede order for apprehension of released expellee?"

A maintenance unit screamed for attention. Liz saw the tiny, spider-like machine edge its way from a tiny hole and make for the command console, where Maran was standing, exhausted and panting from his efforts.

Liz saw with a growing realization that Maran had temporarily disrupted the machines. She could at last begin to reason. Maran was a cyberneticist. Maran understood the mechanisms of control as no one else had ever done. And Maran was loose in a ship which was run by the robots.

Why or how he was loose could wait. That he was loose—that he had begun to exert his bizarre genius over one important system—was enough.

She spoke out, trying to make herself heard over the uproar of the machines: "Get Maran! He's murdered a guard! You two servitors—you had your instructions—get him!"

Sensitive to the human voice, able to select its tones from the robotic clamor, they turned. Behind them Maran reached for a sensor-pad. Liz saw his big head stiffen. His hands moved again, weaving a spell over the command console. Liz might have moved had it not been for the slight disturbance in the ooze beside her.

She looked, the movement catching her eye. The noise of slithering increased. A head peered forward from the gray ooze. Eyes that had been busy with empty dreams were pools of doubt and pain. The prisoner in the ooze was looking at her.

Liz understood what Maran had done to cause such confusion among the robot overseers of the expellees. He had begun to arouse the prisoners. Horrified, she heard Maran's voice. He was calling to the dead man. Recognizing and despising her helplessness, she could only watch.

Maran glanced once, and looked back to the console. The robots' sensors followed his movements but they were still in a state of doubt. Wary, ready to move with smooth speed, they were trapped by the inability of their supervisors to disperse the confusion Maran was still building.

Maran raised his head to take in the scene. Sluggish movements from the tanks attracted him. He began to talk, quietly, soothingly, to the console before him. Within seconds the robotic complaints began to die away. The spider-like robot was a flashing, sparkling thing as it crept toward him. He reached out a huge hand and knocked it away. It lay still.

Rosario had been thinking about Liz Deffant when the first warnings came through. She should have been a bright, talkative, happy girl, but she was not. There was a sadness about her eyes; she had been hurt. Then there was the urgency of her return to Messier 16. Had that something to do with her low-key conversation? He wondered if he could make a stopover on the return flight from the Rim. It might be possible.

The first metallic howls put all thoughts of her out of his head.

The pedestal which housed the *ES 110*'s robotic director let out a blast of protest: "There will be no premature release of prisoners! Instructions are not confused! Galactic Council Penal Code directives are unalterable! There must be no release of expellees until destination reached!"

The normally calm voice was partly obscured by the electronic uproar of shrill systems demanding instructions. Rosario had never heard the robots disagree. This was an emergency, possibly a disaster.

"Release," called Poole, emerging from the dining area. His mouth still champed on food. "Release, Jack! Did it say—"

"Pete!" yelled Rosario into the console before him. "Tup! What's happening down there?"

"A prisoner out," Poole said wildly. "How, Jack, how?"

"Confused data!" screamed a Grade Two robot. "Servitors do not respond to my orders! Prisoner is trying to interfere with controls for this system!"

"The cell-deck Grade Two!" Rosario shouted. "Dieter! Mack!"

The two Security men came at a run. They had no need to be told what was happening. Poole looked helplessly at the console. It was alive with writhing sensor-pads. It seemed demented. Warning lights flashed zanily. A stream of messages clamored for attention. From the Grade One's pedestal came a confused roar of questions. Rosario grabbed a pair of sensor-pads and allowed them to report.

"Do we go down?" asked Dieter when Rosario turned to them.

"No."

"What should I do?" pleaded Poole, infected by terror now.

"Red Alert?" asked Mack.

"It should have gone out!"

"It hasn't?'

"No," said Rosario grimly.

"Then what's happening?" Poole shrilled. "We've an escaped prisoner down there—the Grade Two says so! And he's taking over the deck!"

"What do we have so far?" asked Dieter. He had to shout above the sudden shrilling uproar.

"It's confused, but three different executive systems report the same thing. Whoever's free is trying to reactivate the whole deck. All the cells."

Poole caught the words. "Reactivate, Jack? Who'd do that—no one but a maniac!"

"No one but a person who knew what would send the robots crazy," said Dieter.

Rosario was ahead of him. There was a pattern in the chaotic events. The Grade One robot was appalled. Several of the Grade Two robots had at least temporarily become incapable of decision-making. They had been persuaded to release the expellees. Unbelievable, yet it had happened. Rosario could imagine the scenes on the lower deck as the prisoners awoke.

Neural systems would be receiving stimulative charges. Powerful drugs, heavy electrical bursts, would pour into the conditioned brains of the expellees. Men and women would be shocked into consciousness. Their bodies, totally unprepared for the gross shocks they were receiving, would thrash frenetically in the gray ooze.

"Do something!" bawled Poole.

The robots were in a state of electronic catatonia. They had accepted orders which contravened their code.

"It's him," said Dieter.

Rosario nodded. "No one else. Maran."

"Maran!" Poole squealed.

"We could take him," offered Mack, ignoring Poole's panic.

"No," said Rosario. He knew that three people he knew and liked were in appalling danger. "No," he decided. "We have to stay here and try to get the Grade One to recover. But the main thing is to alert Galactic Center."

"A Red Alert," agreed Dieter.

"With anyone else, we'd try," said Rosario. "But Maran—"

They knew what he meant. Only a Maran could have baffled the sophisticated circuitry of the Enforcement Service vessel.

Rosario turned to the console. "This is Commander Rosario," he said firmly. There was a brief halt in the uproar of metallic protest. "This is a full-scale emergency. Emergency systems must at once beam a request for help. All Service ships in the Quadrant must be informed. Beam the request for help now. A Red Alert condition exists."

"Commander, it is not in your sphere of authority to

decide degrees of emergency," the Grade One robot answered. There was a chilling assurance in its response.

"Beam the request for assistance now," repeated Rosario calmly. "I must be allowed control of the situation. You are receiving false data from a released expellee. I say again, a state of emergency exists. Beam Red Alert signals throughout the Quadrant."

"The situation has been contained. There is no need for alarm, Commander. The expellee has been returned to his coma-cell. He is defunct and will be removed for storage in accordance with Galactic Council Penal Code procedures."

"Someone's dead," said Mack.

Rosario shuddered. Who was it? His mind boiled with anger. But he must keep calm. The machines had been subverted, so much was clear. They were confused. They were making profound mistakes. There had to be a way of making them see the realities of the situation. But what were those realities? What was happening in the cell-deck? Were all the command systems under Maran's spell?

"Well?" asked Dieter, looking at Rosario.

"Not yet. We'll give the machines a chance."

CHAPTER 7

"Excuse me, sir," said the robotic controller of the station. "Commander Buchanan."

Buchanan held his breath. He had seen it. The great leprous blotch made by the uncanny wave emissions from the vast rotating core of the Singularity was now forming into the patterns he had observed three years before.

"A direct sighting, Commander," the robot insisted. "The Singularity."

The profound gap in the cosmos waiting for the unwary. He watched for almost an hour. At last, the ship trembled.

"Commander Buchanan, the tug has released the station. We are now beginning independent flight."

"Yes."

Buchanan watched the tug begin its endless voyage; another drifting hulk that would finish in the interior of some remote star. Then he stared again at the Singularity.

The station would soon be his.

Inside the shocked, pain-filled head of Maran, ideas flared and were instantaneously put into action. He was aware that he was working at a low level of efficiency. The drugs that had revived his body, and the electrical discharges that had smashed through his nervous system, had blotted out whole areas of memory and intellect. Maran knew he was using the dying remnants of his powers instinctively.

The first blinding shock of returning consciousness had nearly killed him. There had been nothing he could do to prepare for it. No barrier could save him from it. The robots would have known if he had kept back the least shred of consciousness. Automatons they might be, but they were superbly designed.

Not until the Enforcement Service ship was way out from Center could the delay-circuit be activated. And when it began its work, when low-grade systems whispered to more sophisticated circuitry, the result was inevitable. Pain, terrible pain. Confusion. Mind-blinding agonies. Perhaps the total dislocation of his faculties. At best, a limited hold on perhaps a quarter of the intellect that had so nearly solved the ultimate mystery. Instinct would have to serve.

It did.

Maran's actions would one day be analyzed in wonder by relays of cyberneticists. There would be fierce controversy over precisely what he accomplished during the first few minutes. Symposia would annually dissect what was known of his subversion of the machines; how remote and unimportant systems were crossed with vital cycles so that the higher control robots would withhold decisions. Maran himself could not have explained.

Dazed, senses screaming in torment, he had emerged from the gray ooze, just as he had foreseen and planned, and moved toward the control console. A memory came back to Maran as he caught sight of the woman. He looked down at his huge hands and felt again the corded sinew of the Security guard's throat. For a moment, he reeled. There should have been no attendants. No guards. His information was that the Enforcement Service ships were entirely automaton-controlled. The guard had not seen him, not even turned. . . .

Maran pushed the memory back into the confusion of his agonized thoughts. The robots must be kept from their appointed tasks—kept in a state of indecision, kept unbalanced. . . . It had been so easy at first. The low-grade servitors advancing, tentacles ready to hold him. And the woman—what was *she* doing on the cell-deck?—stiff with shock! No threat. An alert face, but quite rigid with fear.

The servitors had told him how to handle the situation. "You are subject to restraint order under Galactic Council Penal Code Regulations!" one had said. "You are an expellee and must be returned to coma-cell," another had directed.

Maran's hands had swept over the controls even as other robotic systems reported his actions. No, he had assured the low-grade robots, he was not an expellee. All expellees were in the coma-cells. Expellees could not escape from the cells. It was impossible. So no expellee had escaped. Therefore he was not an expellee.

A query from a Grade Two system which was responsible for monitoring the life-support apparatus of the tanks was answered at once. Maran assured it that all coma-cells were full. There was a prisoner in each of the tanks. Therefore no prisoner had escaped.

Doubly reassured, the low-grade servitors allowed black tentacles to retract.

The girl was recovering, Maran saw. He flinched at the touch of a tentacle. The girl was saying something. She was afraid, but there was the beginning of outraged determination in her eyes. Like all the others, she thought him a monster. Another who could never understand the supreme importance of his destiny. Maran could see the resolve building up in her mind. Others would know that he was loose. They would react more quickly. Crewmen—perhaps more Security guards—certainly a programmed automatic reaction. Then there would be the appeals for assistance, and the big Enforcement Service cruisers would wheel around and follow the wake of the *ES 110.*

Maran's wildly straining eyes took in the rows of gently-bobbing expellees. Their minds were weaker than his. They had frail bodies, some of them. Old men would not stand up to the shocks of sudden revivification. Yet the robots must be halted!

His hands swept down in a dazzling arc. Sensors leaped into his palms. Maran left the high-grade systems bewildered. Bawling metallic voices filled the green-lit cell-deck with a huge uproar. In the midst of it, Maran ordered the release of all the prisoners.

On the deck above, Rosario began to understand the extent of Maran's audacious and brilliant plan. As he struggled to assert some form of control over the machines, Maran poured a steady stream of orders into the Grade Two circuit which controlled the cell-deck. A part of Maran's mind functioned clearly. He could hear Rosario, the commander of the ship. Unlike the robots, Rosario had not panicked. All his energies were going into the one vital response: beaming a Red Alert.

Maran sweated coldly. Black shock waves made him reel. His limbs shuddered. Bunches of nerve-endings throbbed and jerked. He looked up from the console and saw that the girl was almost recovered from the blast of robotic noise. Above, the iron-nerved commander of the ship was talking calmly to the machines:

"This is a full-scale emergency," he was saying. "Emergency systems must at once beam a request for help. Beam the request for help now. A Red Alert condition exists."

Maran waited for the reply to the one message which must not be sent. He heard the Grade One robot's refusal.

The calm voice of the commander did not falter. Maran heard Rosario tell the machine that it was receiving false information: that he had escaped; that he was a danger warranting a Red Alert.

"Check the identity of all expellees," ordered Rosario. "I repeat, check the identity of all expellees held in coma-cells."

The Grade One robot hesitated. Maran acted. Sensor-pads relayed his orders. At the heart of the massive complex of electronic machinery, there was a huge roar of protest. Men and women in the coma-cells twitched, leaped, screamed, thrashed frenetically, slipped back, and died.

"Identity check not possible at this stage," admitted the robotic voice from its pedestal.

Rosario began to realize that he had failed.

"Maran's feeding you false information!" he roared, as the machine whined softly and soothingly. "He's loose—he's confusing you—get him!"

"Try the low-grades," said Dieter. "Appeal to the servitors. They might respond."

Rosario tried. Below, Maran watched as the armored robots listened to the voice of the *ES 110*'s commander. Tentacles flicked out cautiously, then drew back.

"There does appear to be a serious malfunctioning of systems on cell-deck," the robotic controller admitted to Rosario. "One human unit is defunct. I have confused reports and conflicting data."

Maran knew this was the moment of maximum danger.

"Obey me!" called the *ES 110*'s commander. "This is Commander Rosario! All robotic systems should obey only identified Enforcement Service personnel! I repeat, obey only direct orders from Enforcement Service personnel!"

To Liz Deffant, still dazed by the shrieking uproar of the robots, it was plain that Rosario had failed. Maran had managed to obtain control of the cell-deck. And he had convinced the ship's robotic controller that no emergency measures were needed.

"All Grade Three robots to report to the cell-deck," Rosario ordered, with a note of desperation in his voice.

"At once. Use all restraint procedures to hold Maran. Grade Two systems must not, repeat not, allow interference with activation systems. Maintain standing orders. Beam Red Alert to all Galactic Service vessels in range!"

Liz Deffant moved forward a step. It took all her courage, for the slitherings and shrieks from the coma-cells left her frozen with horror. She saw a gaunt head appear over the edge of a cell. Green-black eyes stared at her, pain dazzling them. She stumbled and a hand clawed feebly against hers.

"I have to warn," a calm voice said above her, "that there has been irreparable damage to some human units. This emergency activation procedure is unprecedented!"

Limbs threshed, eyes glared, shrieks were cut off as mouths submerged.

Maran saw the girl moving blindly. She was helpless. His body settled on the command console. Grinding flashes of agony surged through his head. It was the moment of maximum danger, but he grimly kept to his task.

". . . beam the message now! *Now*!" Rosario ordered.

The *ES 110*'s commander was desperate.

Maran heard the cold logic of the Grade One robot as it parroted the answers he had fed into its confused circuitry.

"This system has no procedures for passing to human control, sir. Kindly remain calm!"

"You're in Maran's hands—he's confused you!"

Liz Deffant heard Rosario's voice as if it were a million miles away.

Nothing would stop Maran, she knew. He was fighting for a monumental vision. Not Rosario. Not the unarmed crew. Certainly not the Grade One robot on which, ultimately, the thousands of systems in the ship depended It was under Maran's spell. Liz heard its chilling answers.

"It is essential that expellees be revived," it pondered. "This is an emergency—"

Maran spoke above the metallic voices:

"This is an emergency where normal regard for expellees' welfare must be temporarily suspended!"

The machine repeated his order.

"Yes," agreed Maran, pushing himself upright.

"This is an emergency not requiring intervention or assistance of Service vessels."

Maran encouraged the machine in its decision: "Correct."

"Therefore no Red Alert call need be beamed."

"Jack!" called Liz Deffant. "Jack, can't you get him!"

She could, at last, move. A head looked at her from the ooze. Somewhere a woman's dying screams tore through the low cavern. Liz put her hands to her ears and ran blindly, anywhere to escape from the horrors of the cell-deck. Instinct drove Liz toward the far grav-chute.

Maran was hardly conscious of her. He knew he was at the furthest limit of his physical resources. Above, alert men would be planning to contain him. The machines would soon realign their disrupted programs. Time. He needed time to recover.

Again he instructed the machines. Just before she descended the chute, Liz heard him distinctly.

"There is a possibility of danger for Service personnel on the cell-deck."

"Therefore no Service personnel must be allowed to reach the cell-deck," agreed the almost human voice of the Grade One robot.

"Seal it off," Maran ordered.

"How could he get out?" Poole was saying as the machines decided the fate of the *ES 110* and its strange cargo. "Jack—he couldn't! We'd have known. It would have shown up—the monitors would have picked him up. He would have had to program four major systems, and even then the Grade One would have reported his revival! Jack, are you sure it *is* Maran? Couldn't it be a malfunctioning of the Grade Twos?"

And still they ignored his frightened, reasonable optimism.

"Well?" asked Dieter.

"We're on our own," said Rosario. "No call for assistance went out. I don't know what he's planning—"

Poole was insistent. "You're not listening to me, Jack! I'm the systems engineer! I know what can happen to machines once they start an aberrant pattern—it could all be some kind of interference from—"

Rosario spoke impatiently: "I haven't the time to argue," he said. "It's Maran."

Poole was quiet.

"We'll go down to the cell-deck," said Mack. There was a hard edge in his tone. Dieter looked at his big hands.

"The two of you, then," said Rosario. "I shouldn't ask it."

"He'll be exhausted," said Mack. "Sudden revivifying like that. I don't care what kind of program he fed into the machines to get out. He'll be as weak as a kitten."

"He knows we have to try," said Rosario. "Be careful. And watch out for the low-grades. They'll be alert."

They nodded and turned away. Rosario realized that the time for talk was over. The two Security men were well-trained. But Pete had not stopped Maran. . . . Rosario almost called them back as they reached the grav-chute.

He saw the slight change in the shifting, hazy field that was the entrance to the chute. A robotic voice began to grate out a message. At the same time, Poole ran.

"It can't be Maran!" Poole yelled. "I'll go and put the—"

Rosario added a useless warning. Dieter and Mack had half turned when Poole plunged into the spinning, black-spangled and closing field. There should have been fail-safes, Rosario thought dimly in his last seconds of consciousness. It had all worked for Maran.

Poole's body vanished.

The explosion hurled the two Security guards across the bridge, where they settled slowly. Rosario was partly protected by the pedestal which housed the ship's controller. It began to report on the latest disaster even as Rosario crashed against the console.

It was the nearer of the two low-grade armored servitors that saved Maran. Black tentacles enveloped him and flung him behind a coma-cell. Its occupant was caught by the full force of the explosion.

"Cell-deck sealed off," reported a distant, hollow metallic voice.

"Maintenance units ready to repair blast damage," said another.

"Twelve human units are now defunct," reported a third. "Should this system now discontinue revival procedures?"

The Grade One robot pondered the problem.

"Yes."

There was a cessation of electronic noise. The *ES 110* continued its voyage. The machines waited. Maran, head streaming with blood, twitched in an agonized delirium. After ten minutes, he groaned. The machines tensed.

Their god would speak.

CHAPTER 8

As Buchanan felt the pull of the station's drive, he had to hold down an urge to begin the descent into the maelstrom. He watched the operations screen. The station lay at the rim of the enigma. The three enormous engines surged to erect a force-screen against the insidious and ferocious energies of the strange gap in the cosmos. Buchanan's hands relaxed. For the moment there was power to spare. But enough power? Enough to counter starquake?

It was in the sudden, irregular pulsing of vast gravitational and electromagnetic forces that the danger lay, however. At one moment the station would be riding easily along a simple dipole configuration; and then, in the next minute portion of time, a leaping gobbet of force would blur the simple lines and create an untenable, utterly incomprehensible vortex. And, somewhere within, was the emptiness of the pit.

Deep, unguessably deep.

The ship's scanners sensed the changes in the emissions from the core of the Singularity, but Buchanan sweated coldly each time until the engines responded. The screens held. Perhaps they would continue to hold. But for how long?

The realization came to him that what the station was experiencing was nothing compared to the rushing, monumental cataclysm of starquake.

It was a condition that trapped ships a billion miles from the epicenter of the cosmic storm. And if starquake could draw in powerful ships from such distances, then what forces raged within the Singularity itself? No wonder the robot satellites sent to record the seismic upheavals of the Singularity were lost! What scanners and sensors could begin to measure the raging fury of the interior?

Buchanan began to glimpse the dilemma of the robots.

Nothing in the Galaxy was like the Singularity.

He would proceed with caution.

"We stay at the rim for observation," Buchanan said, awed by a fresh pulsation from the depths.

"That is our assignment," agreed the robot.

Rosario opened his eyes and saw blood. In the bright-lit cheerful surroundings there was a particular horror in the sight of so much blood. Pain came in a dense flood. He closed his eyes, welcoming the darkness. Somewhere near him there was the soft, heavy movement of machinery. Rosario remembered. *Maran.*

He opened his eyes and knew it was his own blood that was congealing on the console. How badly was he hurt? There was a splintered mass of pain down his left side. Ribs gone. He breathed more deeply and the pain engulfed him once again. But he would not permit himself to lose consciousness.

He coughed and the pain surrounded him with armies of dart-wielding enemies. He forced himself to think. He moved his head to see the bridge. *An explosion*, he remembered. A colossal blast. Before that, Poole with his staring, foolish face set in an unaccustomedly determined mask. It was the one truly determined act of his career. And then the molecular spin had taken him apart, grain by grain.

Rosario shuddered. He would have to pass down the chute. Poor, sad-faced Poole's ghost would linger in its force-waves. And then what? What could he do?

Rosario tried to call out. Dieter and Mack . . . had they reached the chute? A Grade Three robot passed before the field of Rosario's vision. He saw that it carried a burden. There was a strong, big-chinned face. The body drooped, inert. *Mack*. Dead.

He forced himself to move away from the console, an inch. It was a desperate struggle. His slowly-growing rage helped keep him conscious. He saw the robot returning for the second smashed body. There was no sign of Poole. There wouldn't be.

Minutes passed, with Rosario hanging by a thread to his sanity. Agony grew in his side like a vast, barbed flower. A Grade Three robot stopped. Rosario felt the gentle touch of a tentacle. He held his breath. The robot inspected him, its carapace shimmering as its sensors absorbed information.

Rosario stared back at it. Was Maran completely in charge of the ship? Had Maran ordered this grisly clearing-up? Or were the machines acting in accordance with their interpretation of standing orders?

He waited.

The robot moved away.

Rosario made himself think. He would have to seek out Maran. Down the grav-chute. Past the remains of Poole. But there wouldn't be any, he thought wildly. Poole was now a part of the fabric of the *ES 110*. Dieter and Mack would be stored away. Then there was Tup.

And the guard, Pete.

And the girl.

And the expellees. Rosario remembered sickly that they had been grotesquely summoned from their remote dreams to help realize Maran's bizarre ambitions. Yes, Maran had gained control of the machines.

Rosario blacked out.

As he lay, half supported by the console, the *ES 110* machines decided that their function was to normalize conditions. Tiny maintenance units cared for their own. The spider-like machines picked up the glittering broken machine which had been knocked away by Maran. Bigger, lower-grade units replaced the smashed panels of the console on the bridge. And a silent corps of servitors began the macabre task of lifting the expellees from the ooze where they had died.

The command system waited.

Rosario again emerged from the darkness and sensed the watchfulness around him. The machines were waiting for instructions. Not from the commander of the Enforcement Service vessel: from Maran.

It had to be now, Rosario told himself. Whatever he had done, Maran was not yet totally the master of the ship. Perhaps he had succumbed to the shock of revivification. Rosario knew what Maran must do now: escape. The ship would leave a wake. Eventually, he must deviate from the huge looping course that would take the ship out to the Rim. When he turned the *ES 110* off-course, robot satellites would register its passing.

But Maran would have time.

Blood gushed from a wide, deep cut at the back of Rosario's head. He felt as if the pain were attacking some other body. Woolly memories baffled him.

"Stand," he said to himself. "Get down to the cell-deck."

"Sir?" asked a passing servitor.

"Carry on," ordered Rosario.

It considered and then moved away. Rosario sweated coldly. He could not ask the machines for help. Not with Maran's insidious instructions subverting the memory-banks of the high-grade systems.

I've got to stop Maran, he thought. He tottered toward the grav-chute. It glowed, promising a gentle descent. The way to the cell-deck was clear.

Rosario looked down at his hands. He was a trained close-combat fighter; not so good as Dieter and Mack, but competent. He almost grinned.

In his state, he might do damage to a frightened butterfly. He could hardly raise his right hand. His left had to hold his wrecked ribs together. He fought down the sick disgust that made him want to shout at his own incompetence. How many had died because he could not assert himself? Why had he not been able to find some counter-argument that would divert the machines from their bizarre decisions?

He looked down at his right hand. It had come down to this. A crippled commander, perhaps the last living member of the *ES 110*'s complement: with one hand. After the utter sophistication of robotic control, a cripple with a head full of pain and one good hand.

The flowing fields of the chute had an insidious attraction. Perhaps even now Maran was coming to meet him.

"No," said Rosario.

He stopped himself. "No," he said, wrenching himself brutally away from the chute. "Not that way."

He braced himself and slowly retraced his steps. Dieter and Mack dead. Poor Poole dying foolishly. Tup—Pete—possibly the girl too.

Yet there could be no question of personal vengeance. Rosario recognized that he had been thinking at a primitive level of consciousness. Not as the commander of the *ES 110.*

He had thought of Maran as *enemy.*

His training had reasserted itself at the last possible moment. It was neither his function nor his duty to attempt Maran's capture.

A tiny flashing maintenance robot crabbed past him. He stared at the opening through which it had come. Somehow he would have to reach the lower levels. A slight disturbance of cold air helped concentrate his senses. He visualized the snaking narrow corridors, dark and chill, which were the arteries of the *ES 110*. Rosario groaned aloud. He was half tempted to make for the grav-chute and the direct confrontation with Maran. But he did not turn back.

Moments passed while he bound his left arm to his body to serve as a form of splint. The light webbing harness was difficult to manage, but at last he had it in place. There was no comment from any of the robots as he slid into the dark hatchway. They were still waiting for Maran to speak.

Rosario wondered if he would live long enough to accomplish his mission. He groped forward. Then he began to slide past conduits, rungs, protruberances, dusty cables and the skittering intent little servo-robots about their blind tasks.

When the blast of the explosion sent a shock wave through the cell-deck, Liz Deffant was already in the lower hold. The noise came to her only faintly. Events had happened so fast, that she had had no time to absorb them. She looked about the bright, cavernous deck, with its rows of gleaming survival-pods, and all was so calm and silent and orderly that she could almost believe she had suffered a phantasmagorical experience. She closed her eyes for a moment.

It was all true. The nightmare was real. She shivered and called out.

It was Al Buchanan's name she called.

She tried to order her thoughts. She saw again the two robots advancing on Maran. Almost, it had been over. They had advanced and then slowed to a puzzled creeping motion. Their tentacles were ready to pinion him, and yet they had halted. Maran's terrible genius had stopped them.

Maran had won, she told herself. But Rosario? Where was he? She had heard him trying to convince the machines that Maran was the danger. He had appealed to them. And all the time, she had been rigid with shock. Why could she not have moved—acted—thrown herself at Maran?

She breathed in shallowly. She was acutely conscious of small sounds that had not been noticeable before. Gentle soft noises. Remote systems pulsating. A distant, heavy jolt from the drive. Behind paneling, slithering movements.

She experienced a moment of panic. She realized that she might be alone. If the *ES 110*'s crew had not yet sought her out, if Rosario had not yet come for her, then they were helpless. Perhaps, by now, they were dead. Then there had been the thin whipping sound as she left the grav-chute. . . .

She was in a torment of indecision and frustration. She looked about the hold. Scores of cylinders flanked the cavern. At the far end a small console stood. In the recess behind it, she saw what looked like a space-lock.

She began to feel a bitter anger. Maran was a throwback to the days of the Mad Wars. He had shown no compunction in sacrificing the lives of the Security men nor the prisoners. Expellees his victims might be—people who had offended so vilely that they were intolerable—but they were human beings. Death should not some so horribly. They should not die so, poisoned in the ooze.

With anger came determination.

What could she do? She was a resourceful woman, but she recognized that she was in a totally unfamiliar situation. Her framework of experience was narrow. She was an ecologist. She had never faced a real danger to her continued existence in her years with the Bureau. And now Maran threatened more than herself.

Maran was in control of a powerful Galactic Service vessel, with all its systems of decision-implementation. She was one person, helpless, unskilled in cybernetics. His sublimely creative mind, which had devised strategies for circumventing the elaborate safeguards of the *ES 110*, was a danger on a colossal scale.

The calm words of Rosario came back to her. *A Red Alert.* That had been the essential thing. Warn the Enforcement Service patrol-cruisers. Warn Center. Tell them Maran was loose. But how?

To allow Maran to continue unopposed was unthinkable. To return to the cell-deck was to invite the fate of Tup and the Security guard. What could she do? Soon, Maran must consolidate his hold on the ship.

He would send out the robots to determine her whereabouts. There would be a little time, probably, before Maran regained his strength. On the cell-deck above, the robots were preoccupied. Until she saw her way clear, she must hide.

But what would that accomplish?

She looked at the nearest survival-pod. Memories struggled for expression. Her determination was growing to an angry resolve, one that could even face the inconceivable. She must halt Maran. Even if it meant returning to the green-lit hell above, she must go back.

She turned to the grav-chute. It gleamed invitingly. But her blood turned to ice and she could not move toward it. She despised herself with a cold fury.

A noise somewhere behind the tall, white cylinders brought her wheeling around. There was movement. Not the noise of servo-systems. Slow, dragging movement, irregular and bleakly menacing.

Liz opened her mouth to scream. She could visualize Maran's massive head, the straining eyes, the ooze-clotted heavy chest. The movement stopped. Whatever was behind the cylinders had sensed her presence.

She backed away.

Then she heard the harsh note of agony. She dared a look back.

She saw a hand, an arm. The rest of the man—it was a man—was concealed. A runnel of blood began to creep from below the cylinder. Liz was poised, either to run or to return. Pity won.

She went back slowly. She saw Rosario's head, with the long wound that was the source of the blood.

In the side of the hold, a narrow panel gaped. There was no movement within it. Nor the least sign of movement from Rosario.

"Jack," she whispered. "You came through *that*?"

He had climbed down some kind of tunnel to reach the hold. She flinched as she turned his head gently. She looked at his body. One arm was bound loosely to his side. The other was stretched out in mute appeal. She had seen serious injuries before. This man needed immediate expert medical attention.

Her first thought was that there would be a surgical unit aboard the *ES 110*. Rosario needed all the care he could get. He might be dying.

She listened for his breath.

There was little enough of it. Liz gulped down a rush of hope. Rosario had opened his eyes.

"I'll get help—"

"No!" His voice was surprisingly strong. "Listen!"

Rosario's head fell back, a dead weight. Even his iron will had its limits.

Another change came over Liz Deffant. First there had been a helpless terror; and then a vague determination that Maran should not be allowed his triumph; now, determination had turned into a clear resolve. She could plan, actively plan. She had remembered something, something that had been swimming in the back of her mind since she had run blindly for the lower deck.

But first, Jack Rosario.

CHAPTER 9

Buchanan felt the station sink down a shaft of strange energies. A skein of hypercubes shimmered dimly on the operations screen. Then they flared into blistering radiance.

"Report!" he ordered.

"Emissions from interior of Singularity increasing in strength," said the robotic controller from its conical pedestal. "Associated discontinuities at edge of Singularity, Commander."

Buchanan snarled suddenly: "I can see that—explain them!"

"Not possible, Commander. The scanners cannot range on the inner core."

"Then range on anything—*anything* that shows up!"

"Yes, Commander."

Buchanan threw the sensor-pads away. They gave him information, but they did not accept his orders. But they would! When the station was affected by the Singularity's weird powers, then the overrider would come into effect. The ship would be his!

He almost missed the sudden image.

"Ships!" Buchanan yelled. *"There!"*

At first he thought he had suffered an hallucination, for the ships—so many of them—seemed to wave and rock as if caught in subtle, shifting eddies. And such ships!

Tiny rocket-craft; here and there a minuscule scouting ship. One giant interstellar colonist ship from the first days of Galactic exploration.

And all of them caught in the writhing coils of the Singularity, all trapped, lost, held cold, dead, forgotten.

The image of the big screen faded even as he spoke, but he had seen them. Yes! Maybe not *the* ship—the one he had come to seek, but certainly ships.

A whole Sargasso Sea of wrecks, held in tenuous force-bands, where they hung in a strange thermodynamic balance—hung by thin timeless tendrils within the eerie depths of the Singularity. Hung in shimmering white-gold tendrils.

Buchanan had seen a score of ships, some of modern design and some grotesquely ancient. Ships that might have trundled from a museum or a fairground.

"Try again!" Buchanan said. "The ships!"

"Ships, Commander?"

"I saw them! It was a steady-state! A gravitational and temporal steady-state! Run the sighting again."

"Not possible, Commander. No sighting was recorded. Steady-state is not an acceptable theory!"

"Not recorded?"

"No, sir." And Buchanan thought grimly of the absurdity of allowing the machines control of anything more complex than a domestic cleansing unit. "This system is not programmed to report and record impossible events!"

It was almost laughable. But life and death were not joking matters. "Impossible—" he said harshly. He stopped.

"Maintain regular scanning."

It was absurd to quarrel with a machine.

Liz Deffant wondered how long they had. Rosario would need food, medical attention, rest.

"Jack! *Jack!*" she called. "The others—where are they?" She put her hand to his lips. She could feel hot dry breath. The solid beat of his heart gave her new strength. There was terrible damage to the rib cage, but he was a powerful man.

There was a faint sound from his lips. The eyes opened again. "Liz?" came the sighing sound.

Rosario's body trembled. Sweat glistened on his wide white face.

"You came down a maintenance shaft—why?" she asked.

He struggled for breath against the anguish of his side. Panic claimed Liz Deffant. She did not want to be alone again. "Jack—*try!*"

He responded. ". . . Center," he got out, lips white. "Warn Center!"

"Yes, if I can! How? What can I do?"

She felt a wild urge to call to the machines for help.

It would take seconds for the servitors to carry Rosario to the surgical unit, minutes to begin the work of repairing the broken bones.

The words froze on her lips. Maran was the master of the machines. To invite their aid was to reveal their presence. But Rosario was dying.

He groaned aloud, eyes open without recognition. He retained enough of his senses to gasp his message, not nearly sufficient to detail instructions. She knew he did not know her, but he must have recognized that she was no enemy, for he said:

"Tup?"

Liz wept bitter tears. "Dead!"

"Pete?"

"Yes!"

"But you—" he breathed, and there was recognition now in his eyes.

"I got away!"

"Warn Center," Rosario said distinctly. "Poole tried—caught in the blast—" Raggedly he went on: "The others—Mack and Dieter—dead!"

Blast? Liz thought, her mind reeling. Blast? She watched Rosario slide into a shallow unconscious state. There had been a thin, whipping sound as she emerged from the chute. Poole dead—caught in the blast? She almost shook Rosario. *"All dead?"*

Liz whimpered with remembered loss. So many grim details crowded her mind now that she could not think clearly. All her earlier resolve seemed to have slid away. It would be easy to close her eyes and sit beside Jack Rosario until the inquisitive robots sought her out. She sat against the hard metal of the nearest cylinder. It would be so easy to rest.

She remained quite still for ten minutes. Nothing at all happened. And then an almost inaudible voice:

"In the pods!" someone was whispering to her. She emerged from a waking dream of fatigue to hear the whisper from white lips. "Liz . . . hurry . . . Maran . . ."

"In the—?"

But Rosario was silent.

"In the pods, Jack? Jack!"

She looked wildly. And remembered.

Survival equipment. Tools — life-support systems — canned air—food—and a medical unit—*a medical unit*!

Liz was confused for a moment. How long would it be

before the robots searched the ship? How long before Maran realized that she had disappeared? Minutes? An hour? Certainly not long! The hunt would be on!

"What shall I do, Jack?"

She had wasted time while Rosario lay dying. She stood up and her mind cleared. The medical unit in the pod. She was no expert, but she had received a basic training in the treatment of injuries. And the medical units contained a guide to treatment. You fed in the observable symptoms and the unit directed your efforts.

She opened the survival-pod.

The individual survival-pods contained life for Rosario. Resolution returned. She knew vaguely that delayed shock had kept her in a trance.

The pods were designed for maximum ease of use.

When the white surface slid away she saw the neat cartons of equipment, supplies, and systems. She reached and took a pack down.

". . . pods . . ." Rosario was whispering.

"Yes!" Liz said, quickly stooping with the medical unit open. Rosario's face was completely gray, with a faint blue tinge at the lips.

She took a knife and cut away his tunic.

Already angry red-blue marks scored his body. He watched, straining for breath. She took a syringe and pumped in the indicated pain-killing drugs. There was a lacy strap that snaked from a container to cling to the man's shallow-breathing body.

". . . listen . . ." Rosario was trying to say.

Liz held another syringe, the one that would bring peace.

". . . don't!" he said with an urgency transcending his torment.

Liz looked at him questioningly.

"Closer," he whispered.

Liz bent. Something in his tones compelled her to delay the beginning of oblivion.

"Liz—use the pod!" he was saying.

"I have! I'll get—"

"No!" said Rosario, faint and with grim intensity.

"What?"

"Use . . . survival-pod . . . gives you a few hours—" He stopped, choking for breath.

Rambling, thought Liz. Confused, hurt, rambling. She would have to hide him.

"Launch!" came Rosario's voice, louder now. His eyes blazed with a passionate urgency. "Use the pod—manual control for launching!"

"What!"

Liz looked about, stunned. Use the survival-pods—while the ship blasted at a staggering speed out toward the Rim?

"Yes! Automatic alarms—Quadrant patrol-cruiser—Red Alert beamed—go!"

"But Maran had the Red Alert canceled!"

"They'll pick up the launch—come to investigate. Go, Liz!"

"An automatic Red Alert beamed when the pod is launched?" Liz said urgently. She had to know.

"Yes—the ship's in deep-space—Phase . . ."

Liz nodded slowly. Maran could be defeated. The cruisers would range on the captured *ES 110* when the pod was launched. They would pick up the automatic alarm.

"Go!" whispered Rosario.

She needed one more piece of information. "Yes, all right, Jack! But how do I launch them?"

Rosario was sinking. "Behind you—manual console—independent—low-grade system!"

"I could use it?"

"Local control—take the pod's designation—feed it in—then 'Release Expellees.' Fifty seconds' delay—then get in the pod—go!"

"Yes," said Liz.

She released Rosario from his agony. His eyes closed. She threw away the syringe. Inside the medical pack she found a stimulant. It acted quickly on her fatigued body. Somehow, she found the strength to push and pull Rosario's body into the survival pod. The dressings about his chest were set like steel. They would protect him. And the drugs would hold him.

"Pod Two-Nine!" she said aloud.

She ran, slipping on the polished floor to the console. It was, as Rosario had said, a simple piece of equipment. A few controls, a single sensor-pad, and a local very low-grade system. Perhaps a Grade Three servitor would normally be given the task of handling it.

The sensor-pad settled limpet-like on her palm.

It indicated receptiveness.

Liz fed it orders.

CHAPTER 10

Maran had been cared for by the robots. They had listened attentively to his hoarse, half-demented ramblings and diagnosed the cause of his condition. His shaking body was taken to the bridge, where surgeon-servitors patched the superficial wounds. Stimulants began to counteract the effects of revivification; fresh plasma replaced heavily poisoned blood; and, impelled by his vast obsession, he began to struggle to full consciousness. He was too late to intervene in the dispatch of the survival-pod.

It was done so quickly that Liz was startled into indecision once more. The console glowed and whined. A port silently slid open. Grabs moved the long white cylinder to the black-mouthed port.

Liz stared about the silent hold. It was time to consider her own position. Hers, Maran's, the ship's. In a moment, Rosario would be ejected in a long, looping parabola away from the *ES 110*. The pod would continue to coast at the speed of the ship, but the small auxiliary engine would gradually take Rosario on a diverging course.

There was a tiny ripple of energy somewhere at the ship's side. Liz felt it. The console reported it. Circuits closed. And a score of higher-grade systems analyzed the launching of the survival-pod. Their evaluation was complete one five-hundredth of a second after Rosario began his unconscious flight.

"Survival-cylinder on flight-path!" reported a metallic voice from the console. "Survival-cylinder launch complete!"

"No expellee-settlement within survival-container's range," another spat back, this one the voice which Liz had learned to recognize as that of a Grade Two executive in the hierarchy of the ship's systems.

"Survival-cylinders are launched only when destination is reached!" the calm, authoritative voice of the robotic controller announced. "There has been a failure of Galactic Council Penal Code instructions! Therefore Galactic Council Penal Code instructions have not been complied with! This automatic control system did not authorize launch!"

Liz felt faint. The machines were puzzled, confused. Like human beings, they sought a scapegoat.

"No systems of Grade Three or above were involved in the launching! There was no failure of automatic control!" the Grade Two executive stated.

Even the small console tried to absolve itself: "This console is not self-programmed nor autonomous, therefore instructions for unauthorized launch did not come from this console."

"Therefore instructions came from some other source!" the Grade Two robot said.

"I am confused!" admitted the Grade One robot.

Liz held her breath. She waited as the machine scanned its memory-banks.

"Survival-cylinder should not have been launched. But cylinder contained expellee! Expellees are not expelled during condition Phase. No expellee has left coma-cell. If no expellee has left coma-cell no expellee is in cylinder. Therefore—" The robot hesitated.

"Survival-cylinder Two-Nine contained a human," said the console meekly.

"Cylinder contained one human!" echoed the Grade One robot. "Unauthorized launching by low-grade system! Therefore request for instructions must be sent to Galactic Center! State of Red Alert exists aboard Enforcement Ship One-One-Zero! Assistance required! Red Alert! Red Alert! Repeat to all Galactic Service ships! Repeat to all Service ships! Red Alert!" the robotic controller called as alarms screamed out.

Liz listened to the exchanges between the machines. She could have wept with relief. Not only was Rosario safe: all around the Quadrant of the Galaxy in which the *ES 110* was warping space aside, ships would be picking up the message and passing it on to the Enforcement Service's patrol-cruisers.

Now she should do what Rosario had told her: program the console to release another survival-pod, the one that would take her away from the terrible Enforcement

Service vessel, its macabre cell-deck, its mute robotic attendants, and the monstrous genius that now controlled it.

Liz took the sensor-pad once more. Its clammy suckers jangled the nerve-endings of her palm. She indicated her wishes.

At once the Grade Two executive declared, from a position at the center of the long, high hold:

"Another survival-cylinder readied for release! Unauthorized launching begins in fifty seconds!"

Liz knew she had little time. She ran to the tall survival-pod. Behind her, there was a clamor of metallic voices. The manual console declared that its program was authorized. Superior systems began to argue. Liz caught a hint of movement from the far end of the hold. A low-grade servitor was watching.

The pod began to close on her.

She stopped it.

There was a strange inevitability about her actions. *Maran*, she said to herself. Maran had a sanctuary. His base had never been found, though the Service had searched the settled Galaxy. Maran was loose and he had a secret, hidden planet where he could continue his experiments: a hidden place, with all his mind-warping machinery intact.

"No," she said aloud.

Quickly Liz Deffant stepped out of the white cylinder. She turned, reached for a heavy package, and touched the survival-pod's manual control. The servitor did not move.

She was just in time. The heavy black grab swung smoothly and silently toward the cylinder. The port at the end of the hold opened.

"Emergency launching!" complained the robotic controller. "Unauthorized launchings of survival-cylinders must cease!"

"I am an ungraded servo-console," said the machine which Liz had programmed. "I have been activated by human personnel!"

"Identify!" the robot controller said.

"Female ecologist Deffant passenger aboard Enforcement Ship One-One-Zero! Deffant has crew status!"

Liz remembered Tup's shy smile. She owed her chance to him. By scheduling her as an *ES 110* crew-member, he had given her an opportunity to avenge his death.

"Female Deffant has authority to launch survival-cylinders!" the Grade Two executive confirmed. "Deffant confirmed as of crew status!"

"Red Alert condition exists," pondered the Grade One controller. "In such conditions human personnel have some executive functions!"

Liz heard the machine's analysis as she ran to the cover of the ranks of cylinders.

It was essential that Maran should believe her to be in the second survival-pod, if only for a few minutes. She knew what she must do. She had always been good with simple machinery.

"The launch proceeds," decided the robot. The port closed silently. The black grab retreated. Liz gasped with relief. The deck shook slightly as the pod winged away from the ship.

"Red Alert condition! Emergency!" bawled the robotic controller. "Survival-cylinder launched prematurely!"

Liz looked down at the heavy package.

She could have been safe by now. The cylinders would last for hours. Maran would not have tried to pick them up. Not with the patrol-cruisers alerted.

Why hadn't she gone?

She knew that she was at the limit of her courage and strength; why not let the Enforcement Service hunt down the *ES 110*?

There was a reason.

Against all odds, Maran had somehow overcome the deep conditioning of the coma-cells. Against all that was reasonable he had managed to avoid the continual monitoring of the machines. His desperate energies had conquered the ship.

Liz was sure, with a deep conviction, that Maran would have a plan to escape the Enforcement Service cruisers. The man was a towering monstrous genius.

She placed the heavy package beside her. She could only hope now that Maran believed her and the rest of the crew dead or gone.

The words on the package gleamed, black on white: *Instructions for assembly of expansion-principle firearm.*

A weapon for use on an unknown planet.

Liz began to strip off the protective packaging.

Buchanan thought of the structure which, in theory, lay at the heart of the Singularity. Strange black hole . . .

cold neutron star: or both? Perhaps neither. If Kochan was right, the Singularity contained the densest matter known. It had more bizarre properties.

To create the rotating vortices of the Singularity, it must have the strangest architecture imaginable; perhaps a form that was beyond conjecture, one that defeated human imagination.

Matter so dense that the enormous contracting pull continued and continued so that all that was left was a hole in the fabric of the Universe.

Matter bent and compressed until space itself parted.

And what when space itself was broken?

It was idle to speculate.

But Buchanan was fascinated by the idea of a black hole in the time-space fabric of the Galaxy. A hole—leading where? Into another framework of space-time that bore no relation to this?

What *was* it that had defeated the robots?

Why were they so sure that the *Altair Star* must join that briefly-glimpsed graveyard of ships?

And why would the robot not acknowledge the existence of the graveyard?

For hours Buchanan ran projections of the framework of the Singularity. He observed roaring upheavals from deep within the writhing Singularity: their source could be small cracks on a crusted core of matter so dense that it would take the energy of a thousand lifetimes for a man to climb a one-centimeter hill on its surface.

And always Buchanan's thoughts returned to his lost command.

He was still in the grip of a somber vision where the survivors of the *Altair Star* hung in an undead limbo when a new robotic voice clamored for attention:

"Galactic Alert! Galactic transmission on Red Alert channels! I have a message with top priority for all ships within this Quadrant, Commander Buchanan!"

"Let's have it," he said. It must be important. Red Alerts went out for full-scale disasters. They took precedence over all other beamed communications.

"Enforcement Ship One-One-Zero reports unauthorized handling of automatic systems. All ships scan for position and course! Do not approach! Enforcement Service cruisers are now proceeding to intercept!"

Buchanan could imagine the scene aboard the vessel. A failure of a robotic monitor. Nothing serious, but the machines would take no chances with the resourceful, vicious, opportunistic men and women who had been expelled from the settled worlds.

Buchanan shrugged.

There were fail-safes. The Enforcement Service had never lost a ship.

It was not his problem. The cruisers would soon reach the Enforcement Service ship.

"Scan," he ordered, forgetting that the robot controlled his ship.

"It has been done, Commander."

"And?"

"No readings," the robot controller said at once. "No contact with *ES 110*."

"We're not specifically asked to take action?"

"My Grade One colleague made no mention of action other than repeating the report."

"Then I need do no more?"

"Nevertheless, Commander—"

"Leave it to the Service."

"There was a full-scale Red Alert—"

"Forget it!"

"I can hardly do that, sir!"

"Keep me informed," Buchanan said. Old habits of command died hard. So did the deep-held sense of responsibility that came with the years of Galactic Service.

"Very good, sir."

Buchanan looked about the bright deck. The *ES 110* was not his concern.

"Let me see the Singularity again."

"Yes, sir."

Buchanan dismissed the prison-ship and its minor problems from his mind. Before him flowered the wispy outline of the Singularity. He marveled at the flow of energies within its depths. Magnetic fields a trillion times larger than those in powerful stars boiled in its rotating interior.

If some combination of black hole and neutron star configuration was the epicenter of the starquakes that shook the cosmos around the Singularity, then the station might well be in peril.

He would not be deterred.

More than ever now that Kochan's team of scientists had come up with a new and utterly strange idea of an eternal moment of death, he was determined to enter the uncertain dimensions.

Maran flung away the skeletal arm of a robot attendant as he emerged from unconsciousness. He had been in a state that was not sleep, but one which allowed him to dream. It seemed that he was back at the start of his experiments. Men and women he had known drifted into his thoughts, calling to him that the ultimate mystery lay only just beyond the moment. They were proud, almost arrogantly proud, to have joined him. A little more perseverance, they called; another, more searching, machine that would rip through the layers of consciousness and point to the primal source of intelligence. They vanished in a blaze of light as he opened his eyes.

Almost instantly he knew the long months of planning might be so much wasted effort. He blinked, pushed away the restraining arm of the robot, and felt strength pulsing through his big body. His mind was startlingly clear, so different from the pain-racked half-mind of those ferocious moments as he crawled from the ooze. . . .

He said aloud: "The crew!"

"No emergency exists," a fairly high-grade system was saying. "Therefore no further Red Alert calls need be beamed."

"Red Alert—" Maran roared. *"A Red Alert?"*

"In the absence of instructions to the contrary, sir," began the smooth voice from the pedestal, "this system took it upon itself, in accordance with programmed data, to beam signals to—"

"Leave it! Why send the Alert?"

"Second survival-cylinder launched!" a Grade Two system announced.

The robotic controller added its own comment, without answering Maran's question: "Therefore a Red Alert signal must be beamed!"

"No!" Maran shouted. "No emergency exists! Do not beam any signals without my express authorization!"

"Therefore no Red Alert signal need be beamed," agreed the Grade One robot calmly. "Because a survival-cylinder was launched during condition Phase, sir, it was necessary to send the programmed signal to all Enforcement Service vessels. That is why the Red Alert signal was beamed, sir. Does that answer your query satisfactorily?"

It had gone wrong. In spite of all his careful planning, there had been flaws. Enough of the crew had been left to summon aid. Maran cursed his lack of strength. If he could have kept fully conscious for a few more moments!

The machines were ready to block off the crew from any part of the ship's controls. He had held the *ES 110* in his hands. And he had weakly succumbed to the revivification process. But it was only to be expected.

There was a long silence. Maran could sense the agony of the machines. They had been told to disobey their deeply-implanted programs. Many of the systems would have suffered irreparable damage. He reached for the sensor-pads which writhed obediently as he demanded information.

He learned of Poole's ironical end. The unknown crewman had given him the respite he had so badly needed. Reluctantly, the memory-banks added details. There were no living crew-members aboard the *ES 110*. Its commander, Rosario, had been badly injured, but he had struggled to the hold.

"Commander Rosario," said Maran. "Where is he now?"

"The commander is at present in a survival-cylinder approximately eighteen million miles from—"

"Gone!"

"Yes, sir." The Grade One robot almost groveled. "It contravenes Galactic Council Penal Code instructions to dispatch cylinders during condition Phase, but in emergency certain procedures may be deemed necessary—"

"Leave that." He thought for a moment. "Could we pick him up?"

"Of course, sir! However, it is probable that the nearest patrol-cruiser will be able to reach him in less time."

"Cruisers," said Maran. Of course there would be cruisers. It would have been easy to avoid the satellites which were strung out so sparsely in the voids between the spiraling arms of the Galaxy. He could have vanished, along with the powerful ship. Now, the Enforcement Service ships would sniff him out.

The big prison-ship would leave a warp-shift clear across the dimensions. Its wake would last for a hundred years. Maran knew enough of deep-space ships to realize that the cruisers' task was simple. They would follow the *ES 110* with the assured ease of hunting dogs.

The machines tried to please. Now that Maran was functioning, they were his willing slaves.

"Beam picked up by Service vessel, sir," the Grade One robot reported. "Instructions? Scanners report second survival-cylinder beam also reaching cruiser."

"Second cylinder?" Maran said. In the moment of

realization that the alert had been beamed, he had overlooked the report of a second launching.

The Grade Two system hastened to explain: "Second survival-cylinder also launched by female Deffant. But no Red Alert condition now exists," it added defensively.

Maran remembered the shocked face of a young woman. The eyes glowed with intelligence, though, intelligence and resolution.

"She was a crew-member?"

"Miss Deffant had crew status," obliged the Grade One robot. "She had authority to launch the cylinders."

"Miss Elizabeth Deffant is an employee of the New Settlements Bureau," added a lower-grade system.

"So she got herself and Rosario away," Maran said aloud. She was resourceful.

"No, sir."

Maran checked as he was about to order a change of course. "Rosario is in one cylinder?"

"Yes, sir."

"And in the other?"

"It was released empty, sir."

"Where is she?"

The machines were silent. Maran ordered a search of the vessel. The orders were delegated to servitor-scanners. There was an atmosphere of quiet cooperation, complete subservience, and some apprehension in the ship. The robots sensed Maran's dissatisfaction.

Sight orifices explored the recesses of the ship.

"Female Deffant is on the survival-deck," a Grade Two system announced. "She gave authority for release of two cylinders. This is a direct contravention of Galactic Council—"

Maran waited with an intense patience. Ideas thronged his busy mind. He thought of the vast, boiling wake left by the *ES 110*. He could visualize the gray-black snouts of the cruisers as they arrowed onto that flooding wake. Somewhere, two cylinders tumbled and eddied among the storms of hyperspace. Gradually, the ideas became coherent.

"Miss Deffant is leaving the survival-cylinder hold," the Grade Two system announced.

Maran waited. It was impossible—a lone woman?

"Female Deffant is on the cell-deck!"

The robot was incredulous.

CHAPTER 11

"The assignment is one of observation, not investigation, sir! I have to remind you—"

Buchanan suffered the arguments for five minutes. It was right. The machine was programmed to remind him of his primary task. Then he grew tired of argument.

"Now."

He was too tense to relax in the comfortable command-chair. Ratlike sensors writhed into his palms. And still the robotic controller pointed out that it was his task to report on the Jansky Singularity, not to enter it.

"I am assuming command," he said. "No more questions, no more advice."

"Sir—"

"The station is within the Singularity's parameters."

"This Grade One robot agrees," it said reluctantly. "Therefore command decisions rest with the commander of the Jansky Singularity Station. And you, Commander Buchanan, are the commander of the Jansky Singularity Station."

"In. Now."

"Yes, sir. According to your instructions."

It was the *Altair Star* engulfment all over again. Buchanan waited, filled with dread, fearing more than death. But huge engines surged to combat the grip of the Singularity's fields. The station flicked inward, rolling into the rotating, glowing phenomenon. Shields sprang out to counteract grotesque forces.

The station vanished into the Singularity.

Across the spiraling arms of the Galaxy, long gray cruisers turned and activated drives seldom used. They blasted through endless reaches of infragalactic space, across the starways of the dimensions and clear through to the gulfs where two survival-cylinders drifted in the wake of the *ES 110*.

The commander of the nearest cruiser gave sharp, terse orders. The spaceways began to empty. Passenger liners wheeled away into safer regions; colossal cargo-ships ten miles long and crewed by servo-robots lumbered out of the cruisers' field of fire; tiny yachts shot into contiguous quadrants yapping out irate questions. There were no answers.

Soon, the gray-black snout of the cruiser drifted near the slowly-tumbling cylinders. Force-fields sprang out and the enigmatic pods were drawn inboard, still flooding the beamer-channels with their siren-blasts: *Red Alert! Red Alert! All Enforcement Service ships rebeam! Red Alert!* The noise was cut off abruptly. Three cruisers could handle anything known in the Galaxy, possibly in the Universe. They were the striking force of the Service. Their armament was always in a state of readiness.

Tensely the crew waited as armored robots filleted the survival-pods. They took no chances. Blast-walls protected them, radiation-suits encased them; and it was left to the servo-robots to recover the contents of the pods. But when they saw the badly-wounded man, immobile, drugged, half conscious but still struggling to frame his message, they raced to him.

He said one word, but that was enough. Loaded with partially-suppressed agony, he breathed: *"Maran!"*

And then he began his fight for life.

The ship's commander, a tall gray-haired man whose days in the Service were almost at an end, did not reveal his thoughts as he gazed at the leaden, shrunken face.

"He'll make it," offered the medical officer.

The commander nodded.

"If he says anything else, let me know."

A youngish lieutenant burst out: "Why wasn't there anyone in the other pod—why two of them? How could Rosario have launched two pods?"

The commander was thinking of Maran. Maran loose: free to begin that frightful series of neural operations. . . .

"We'll know when we reach the *ES 110*," he told the young officer. He crossed to the gray metal, coldly-functional console. Robotic servo-mechanisms sensed his nearness and awaited his orders. The cruisers were the only ships programmed for complete and unquestioned control by human personnel. There were those in positions of power who questioned the wisdom of risking fallible human discretion, but the members of the Service had so far persuaded the Galactic Council that the robots could not cope with the situations in which they might find themselves. They had not the resources for the kind of decision that occasionally must be made.

The commander spoke to his field man: "Link with the squadron. Try a combined submolecular field. I want the ship intact."

Liz Deffant's hands were steady as she pieced together the surprisingly elaborate mechanism. Several screws had to be wound into place. There was a sighting apparatus—merely a notch, but it would be adequate. The weapon had a short range. About a hundred yards, Liz guessed. A small hammer held the flint. There were springs, ratchets, a flashpan. All had to be in alignment.

The propulsive force was a black powder, a mixture of easily-available chemicals. Out at the Rim, the expellees would have no difficulty in locating sources for the primary materials. Before a year or so passed, they would be able to manufacture simple tools like this for themselves.

Pour the grains of powder into the upturned barrel of the weapon, she read. She split the cartridge and made a wadding from the cartridge-paper.

Prime the weapon by placing a pinch of powder in the priming-pan. Liz wondered if her fingers were sweating too much. She wiped them free of moisture. A misfire could occur; she would have only one chance, for the process of preparing the weapon for firing had already taken over a minute.

Tap the projectile into the barrel, using the ramrod. Take care not to distort the shape of the projectile.

The bullet rested on the wadding. All about her, Liz sensed the interest of robot eyes. She could have wept with fear. It was an absurd situation, ridiculous. A chance encounter with a friend of Al's had led to this distillation of terror, to this gagging range of emotions which had previously been unknown territory. She was bitterly afraid. The determination that had kept her from leaving the *ES 110* was almost entirely dissipated. She could not begin to understand why her fingers continued to prepare the barrel-loading, archaic musket, for there was no directing force behind the movement.

They were a part of a pattern of events which had

encompassed her. She felt as if she, too, were a part of the robotic equipment of the prison-ship, a preprogrammed and mindless complex of nerve and tissue that was a part of the spatial and temporal framework of events beginning with the sight of Tup's dying face, and taking in the horrors of the past few hours. The situation had grown around her. She had grown into it. There was a terrible inevitability in it.

She took the heavy weapon, careful to close the priming-pan. Tears streamed down her face as she began to walk toward the wide grav-chute. It led to the clamorous horror of the cell-deck, to the puzzled low-grade servitors, to the tanks where the expellees writhed, and to the splayed, silent body of the naïve crewman she had known as Tup. And, somehow, she could negotiate the silent, eerie green-lit deck.

The robots had finished their work. Many tanks were empty. The dead crewmen were gone. She knew that unseen scanners reported her presence. Twice she saw groups of low-grade servitors, but they did not attempt to hinder her.

She had known at once that Maran would not be on the deck. She grasped the musket in almost nerveless fingers, feeling the smooth stock, the heavy barrel, the delicate priming mechanism. Icy sweat covered her face and hands. Maran would be on the bridge.

"Al, I wish we hadn't parted like that," she whispered. When she began the quick ascent to the bridge, she could recall every line of his face. She had stormed away from him filled with a bitter rage, and she could see now the poignant hurt in his eyes. The sense of loss was almost unbearable.

After the green-lit half-light of the lower deck, the bridge was startlingly bright.

Liz Deffant stepped out of the chute, narrowed her eyes against the flooding light, and sought out Maran. The musket almost slipped from her hand. Two things immediately impacted on her mind: two low-grade servitors were very close to her; and Maran stood squarely before her, outlined against the bulk of the robotic controller's pedestal. He seemed to have been waiting like that for aeons.

His great body was clad in black. There was a half-smile on his face, so that Liz had the feeling that he would come toward her almost indulgently. His eyes were nearly beautiful, she thought inconsequentially, more a woman's eyes than a man's. His eyebrows were perfectly curved above the heavy-lashed, wide-set eyes.

Liz raised the musket and, enwrapped in her strange trance, she had a prevision of a third eye opening redly above the pair that were regarding her. The projectile was heavy, round, metallic and in a tenth of a second it would smash through the large skull and Maran would be no threat to anyone. The trigger curved in a bow against her finger.

Maran made a small gesture with his large, white hands. Liz had the impression of ponderous movement. The sights of the weapon were exactly aligned on the center of Maran's forehead.

Maran said with massive calmness: "Miss Deffant, do you really know what—"

The rest was lost.

She flicked the priming-pan open, noticed in a frozen moment of time that a few grains of powder had clung to her damp fingers, and then she pulled with increasing power on the trigger. The flint snapped down.

Fire blossomed, red and yellow. Smoke gushed from the priming-pan and the barrel, and Liz was hurled backward by the recoil. She did not know whether she was glad, relieved, horrified, amazed, or empty of emotion.

The smoke cleared.

Maran had not fallen.

The clear brown eyes were not glazing in death, as the young crewman's had. And there was no third eye. Liz knew cold, clawing fear.

She stepped back half a pace, her shoulder raw and full of pain, and then she could not step back. A black tentacle carefully detached her hands from the metal of the musket. Maran came toward her, and Liz opened her mouth in pure, blind panic.

She could hear the echoes of her scream bounding back from the cheerful pastel-colored walls. When she moved, delicate tentacles restrained her. And Maran stopped.

The half-smile had gone. There was a look of sadness on his face, that of a large man who knows that, in spite of his harmless nature, the sheer physical bulk of his body inspired fear in others. Liz held onto her sanity, gagging down her bile. She realized that he was talking to her.

"Miss Deffant," he was saying for the second or third time. "Miss Deffant—was it you who released the survival-cylinders? Miss Deffant?"

Liz repressed a shuddering sigh. He would want his revenge. The man was a merciless, obsessed psychopath. All human emotions had died within him; he lived only for some bizarre vision. And this was the man she thought could be right about the need for investigation into the nature of the only intelligent life in the Galaxy. She wondered if he would kill her now.

"Yes!" she spat at him. "I did it—and the whole Quadrant is repeating the Red Alert! Every Enforcement Service ship in the fleet will be after you!" She almost dared him to kill her, but she could not. There was too much animal fear in her. She could not challenge him so directly, not after what he had done so easily to the guard and the young crewman. She could only wait.

"It was the bravest thing I've ever known," Maran said.

Liz shuddered, awaiting a blow, the condemnation to some vile form of death, instructions to the robots to dispose of her—for anything but this. What had Maran said? That her action was the bravest thing he had ever known? He was sincere.

There could be no doubt, for his face expressed only an admiring interest. The grim mask she had first seen glaring wildly about the green-lit hell of the cell dock had changed into this benevolent visage. Maran was looking at her with the indulgent air of a schoolmaster glad that his pupil had absorbed her lesson well.

"I tried to kill you," she heard herself whispering.

"Yes."

"The cruisers will take you." Liz felt again the uncanny sense of detachment from the situation. It was almost as if the words were spoken by another woman.

"Possibly," Maran said.

"They will!" She could challenge him now.

"Quite possibly, Miss Deffant." He was quite calm. Liz could begin to understand the power of the man. He was massively indifferent to her attempt on his life.

Shuddering afresh, she said: "I would have killed you."

"You thought I was some kind of monster."

He accepted it. Tears trickled down Liz's face and she

was bitterly ashamed of herself for them; for she knew that they came with the relief of knowing that she would not be killed. Maran would not harm her. The great white hooks of hands would not reach out. . . .

"Sit down, Miss Deffant. You are almost exhausted. If you make no sudden move toward a possible weapon, the machines will ignore you."

"They stopped me from—"

"I watched you come from the lower deck, Miss Deffant. I wondered if you would have the courage to carry through your plan." The great brown eyes were full of warmth. "The servitors were programmed to disturb your aim only if it was accurate. It was." He pointed to a white metallic scar above him. Liz could see the long line of the leaden projectile splashing the ceiling with its track. She sat down, aware of Maran, of the robots' careful scrutiny, of her own shaking hands; and also of her own resignation.

A voice that she knew as her own said: "Did you have to kill them?"

Maran sighed. There was an indisputable sadness in his voice, a real regret in his face when he answered.

"When I was able to get out of the tank, I was still in a deep conditioning, Miss Deffant. You were right to be afraid when you first saw me. That was a monster, that creature who destroyed two lives—when threatened, it acted at the most primitive level in the most direct way." His eyes were hypnotically attractive. Liz felt her anger dying away. "That creature is gone, Miss Deffant. You see before you only—Maran."

And he was not looking at her, but through her. She sensed the evocative power of his name: repeating his own name had a talismatic effect. It reestablished him, gave assurance to his remote and majestic vision, substance to his belief in his rightness, in his destiny. Liz shivered. A pale reminder of her furious determination echoed in her mind: she had known that Maran would have a plan to evade the cruisers. That was why she had assembled the archaic firearm from the survival-cylinder; even now Maran's incredible mind would be building a strategy for survival. And there was nothing she could do, nothing at all.

And there it was, thought Buchanan. The electromagnetic conundrum, the gravitational enigma, the terrible

Singularity, that contained the most bizarre architecture of any object in the Galaxy. Around the station, pulsing with incomprehensible powers, the core of the Singularity set in motion force-fields that were beyond measurement.

Buchanan held back a prayer as the three huge engines bit into the straining coils. They gripped the station. Buchanan could feel the very deck beneath him curving slightly in response to the gigantic flood of power from the three pods. The engines surged, bit, and the serpentine coils relaxed.

The coils glistened. They backed away like scorched snakes.

The makers of the station had foreseen the uncanny power of the Singularity. The engines surged again. And they held the web of coiled forces emanating from the darkness at the center of the Singularity. The screen of the station projected red-banded submolecular fields, and Buchanan wiped the sweat from his face. He watched and lost himself in the marvel of the machines.

The Singularity was an imponderable, a freak. But human ingenuity had defeated the fantastic vortex. The small, squat, ugly vessel hung at the edge of Beyond. But it was not drawn into the gaping maw of the terrible Singularity. It survived.

It had survived, thought Buchanan, with a sudden accession of pride. The Jansky Singularity Station truly existed! Built with a single purpose in mind, it was a technological marvel. But a marvel of limited scope. Three colossal engines, each enough to power a vast infragalactic ship. Stupendously overpowered, absurdly potent.

None of this power usable in warp-shift, all of it directed toward containment. To hold back the forces of black night. To keep the station swanning through the edges of the Singularity. And more, thought Buchanan. It had done more. Even within the Singularity, the station was safe.

Its shields could divert the stupendous and bizarre vortices of the Singularity. They heaved, struck, and glissaded away. The station slid out of the serpent's coils.

Buchanan experimented with the strange dimensions.

The station clawed into a furious maelstrom.

Buchanan's senses reeled as the ship was flung about in the depths. He eased the ship into a calmer region. The robot controls in his palms translated his commands into action. Creaking with monstrous powers, the engines held a strange equilibrium in the weird inner depths.

Then Buchanan saw what he sought.

"Dear God!" he whispered as the maelstrom's fantastic energies fell away and he saw into a corridor of unholy calm. "The ship!"

It was the strange graveyard of ships he had glimpsed before the descent into the Singularity. And there was his lost command!

He sweated as the screened image of the *Altair Star* was steady for long moments. The ruin held a lonely, frozen space among the other ships of long ago. The scanners ranged closer. He could see details. There were the marks of that ferocious wrecking when the bridge was ripped away. An engine hung clear of the ship, torn away as if by a kraken. But what of the silent crew and passengers? What of the silent company of the dead? Or the undead!

"Readings!" he snapped to the robotic controller. "How near—how soon!"

"Sir?"

"The *Altair Star*—there!"

"This automaton installation has records of the *Altair Star* lost three years ago. You want the details, Commander?"

It knew, of course, of his past. The machines had their own subtle ways of passing on information. The Grade One system that was now at his command knew quite well that he had once been the chief officer on the *Altair Star*.

"She's there! You must have readings—I can see it on the screen! The scanners must have assessed the parameters! I'm sure it's a steady-state!"

"No data, Commander," the machine said.

Buchanan grew angry. The machines were ranged against him.

"I can see it! You must have readings!"

"Of what, sir?"

"The *Altair Star*!"

"No readings, Commander."

Buchanan contained his excitement. He determined on reason rather than rage. You couldn't hate machines. You could try not to. In fact, you could not manage without them, he told himself. However much you could do on your own, you needed them, every last system of the millions aboard the station. *Understand the robot,* Buchanan ordered himself. Why was it refusing to admit the *Altair Star* lay within the deep well of the Singularity?

The sensors in his wet palms fed in continuous streams of information: the ship's energy levels; the reserves of power available in the three great engines; estimated characteristics of electromagnetic forces emanating from the center of the vast web of the Singularity. Nothing on the eerie tunnel that contained the ships!

"Scan!" ordered Buchanan again. "There!"

The screen changed at his direction. Buchanan ranged closer. The *Altair Star*'s hulk came nearer. He could make out details of ports and scanner-housings. And something else. All about the ship was a glistening cocoon of black-gold pinpoints of light.

"Still no readings?" asked Buchanan.

"Of what, Commander?"

"The *Altair Star.*"

"The *Altair Star* was a total loss, Commander."

"Even though I can see it now?"

The machine was silent for minutes. Buchanan could imagine the endless circuits far below him, all searching for an answer. At last it spoke, and again the Grade One robot retreated into unknowledge.

"This installation cannot register the impossible, Commander."

"Impossible," breathed Buchanan.

The strange graveyard that existed within the rotating fury of the Singularity was impossible.

And yet it lay there, in an eerie matrix of forever.

But the robots could not—would not acknowledge it. The strange timeless tunnel did not exist. It was impossible.

So it did not exist.

How could he convince the machines otherwise? If he were to go closer, he needed the massive resources of the station's robots. He needed the robots and their instant technology.

Warning impulses roared through the nerve-endings of his palms. He ignored them, mesmerized by the sight of the *Altair Star*. He had to get aboard that ill-fated vessel!

"Commander Buchanan!" the robotic controller called. "High field momentum from the Singularity core! Action necessary!"

Buchanan still watched, and it was only when the frosted, glittering *Altair Star* began to disappear behind strangely alive coils of imponderable forces that he shook himself free of his ghost-ship's spell.

"Well?" he asked.

"Commander Buchanan, core emissions indicate maximum danger."

The station juddered as its screens adapted themselves to the huge energies flowing from the bizarre center of the Singularity. Buchanan saw the screen shiver and dissolve. The scanners roved the Singularity.

Then Buchanan lost interest in the *Altair Star*, for a probing scanner ranged deep into the central core.

He saw into the very womb of Singularity, the hole that gave birth to the wild, incomprehensible and deadly monster that dominated the Quadrant.

"The hole," whispered Buchanan.

Seemingly empty, black, formless, and yet having properties of shape, it was a gap that held neither time nor space.

"Go!" Buchanan called, suddenly more afraid than he had been for three years. "Go!"

"Starquake," commented the robotic controller. "Commander Buchanan—starquake! The station is in danger, sir!"

Still awed, Buchanan punched orders into the console.

The station's three storehouses of energy screamed with effort. Roaring, pulsing, blasting, they countered the ferocious unguessable emissions from the black hole. Yet Buchanan still watched that uncanny gap in the cosmos, even as the station began to slide away from the seismic disturbances.

He held the scanner locked onto the eerie black hole until the station abruptly bit with great fangs into the serpentine coils that embraced it.

Slowly the station heaved itself away from the furious storms of the inner depths. It clawed out and away from the frightful emissions.

Buchanan could still see that terrible emptiness long after the scanner was unable to range on it. The black hole had imprinted itself on his mind; it was an afterimage on the retina, one that would not leave him.

There was a cosmic mystery here: Buchanan was almost stupefied by the otherness of what he had seen.

The black hole belonged to no part of the Galaxy.

It was the ultimate mystery, the ultimate danger. Buchanan felt drained, spent, utterly fatigued.

Some hours passed before he could concentrate on his self-imposed task. Buchanan slowly recovered. There was no slackening of his resolve. Starquake had not dismayed him. The eerie black hole had left him shocked but not overwhelmed. The strange graveyard was terrifying, but he could face it. Buchanan looked at the robot's cone-shaped pedestal.

Somehow he had to convince the machines that what he had seen was possible. That the huge Sargasso Sea and its wrecks were not beyond reach.

There was one source of comfort. The station had proved itself. Even the frightfulness of starquake could not dent its shields. They had held, just as the engineers promised. But God help any ship that came near the Singularity now!

CHAPTER 12

"Enforcement Service cruiser ranging. Course altering. Super-Phase engaged," reported a scanner.

They would have picked up Rosario, thought Liz Deffant. She sat quite still in the comfortable, deep seat as Maran soothed the disturbed high-grade machines. She had expected pain and terror, grotesque threats, Maran's fury. And nothing had happened. Her reaction had been predictable, she recognized: resignation and a state of complete supineness. Not only did she feel that she could no longer interfere in the take-over of the *ES 110*: if there had been a practicable way of upsetting Maran's schemes, she could not have brought herself to consider it. She was drained of nervous energy. *Shock*, her mind said again. *You're in shock*. The shock of Maran's totally unexpected treatment. He was a murderer, yet he had a strange dignity. He was a warped personality, yet he could talk sanely to her about her work with the New Settlements Bureau though three cruisers were ranging on the *ES 110*.

"You're with the exploration teams, Miss Deffant," he had said encouragingly. "I expect you know the planet where it was intended to send me?"

"Not that one. Not personally. I know of it."

She had been able to answer in the same calm way. And what a conversation it had been. Herself, scared witless and only now able to control the shaking of her limbs; Maran, almost elegantly directing the machines that had once controlled the *ES 110*. Here she was on the bridge with a huge, black-clad man who regarded her with compassion and admiration. Maran the murderer. Maran whose bizarre machines had ripped out the minds of so many deluded men and women.

"I believe it's an inhospitable planet," he was saying, talking as if she were a respected colleague, discussing the planet at the Rim where this batch of expellees would have been ejected.

"It was tolerable," she said. "A rather severe range of temperatures. But there were excellent indigenous building materials. There was a problem with carnivores—" She stopped. She was replying to him as if he were not the murderer of the guard and poor dead Tup. Maran saw her hesitate.

"Hence the primitive ballistic missile-projectors in the pods," he prompted. "Resourceful thinking, Miss Deffant."

"You killed them!" Liz burst out, unable to sustain the role Maran was offering her.

"Regrettably, yes." Maran turned to the console and fed in commands. He turned back to look at her. "But for you," he said slowly, "I could turn this ship toward my own planet. Maran could begin again. Everything is ready." Liz flinched as she saw the muscle straining in his neck. He was flabby, but the muscle was there. "Now, Maran must run."

"I'm glad!"

"Naturally, Miss Deffant. But you must agree that you have caused me considerable harm."

"Message beamed from Enforcement Service cruiser," interrupted the Grade One robot. "Commander Lientand requests direct visual and sound contact with crew-members. Failing that, sir, he requests similar contact with you."

"You can't possibly get away," Liz said quietly. "Not three cruisers—it just can't be done. Talk to them. They'll try to understand."

It took all the strength she could summon up, this plea to Maran. She was fascinated by his impassive gaze. He was looking past her now, to the big operations screen which showed a shadowy representation of the gray-black form of the cruiser. The blue-pulsing screen was the center of all his thoughts. It seemed that he was willing some new contingency to arise. Liz had the feeling that, if he stared hard enough at the operations screen, some avenue of escape would open in the blank reaches between the arms of the Galaxy.

"Three cruisers now on converging course," reported another scanner.

"There's nowhere to go," Liz said, more softly still.

"We leave a wake like a comet's tail," said Maran. His

big white hands flickered over the console. Liz saw the cosmos pinwheel on the big blue operations screen.

The entire Quadrant lay before her. Another sensitive motion of Maran's hands brought the coruscating wakes of three cruisers into brilliant focus. "The cruisers," said Maran, and the long black snouts had the look of night creatures. "I wonder if they know you are aboard?"

"Talk to them."

"No, Miss Deffant." And now he looked at her directly. "I wonder if they know you are aboard the ship?"

Liz said scornfully: "A hostage! They won't worry about one Bureau employee—not now they know you're loose! They'll do anything to stop you!"

But Maran was not listening to her.

"Another request for reciprocal voice and vision contact, sir," the Grade One robot said deferentially.

"No," said Maran. "There is no need to accede to the request."

"There's no likelihood you can use me as a hostage," repeated Liz. "What good can it do to try to escape?"

Maran was intent on the screen. She had ceased to exist for him.

"Time," he muttered. "Time! It's possible, but once they know, they can range on the ship!"

Liz felt blackness crawling into her head as Maran suddenly jerked the enormous Enforcement Service ship out of its course and plunged it wildly among the storms of hyperspace. Gold-shot sable-edged shards of jangling molecules slipped through her brain-cells, leaving an impression of pure chaos. The robots howled reports. Alarms screeched out across the bridge.

Momentarily, Liz saw the cause of Maran's lightning action.

The three cruisers had turned in a skilled and predetermined move, each flinging out a vast skein of force-fields to inhibit the *ES 110*'s drive. Traceries of power flashed toward the ship in a careening, terrifying onrush of pyrotechnics. Maran had seen the maneuver. And he had evaded the cosmic whirlwind.

"Evasive action!" the robotic controller called. "This ship must take evasive action against Enforcement Service cruisers' apprehend procedures! Why?"

Maran punched commands and it was silent.

Liz was deep in the shelter of a soft couch, whose restraint bands had automatically cocooned her against the violent forces surrounding the ship. Maran's bulky strength kept him at the console, the command chair enfolded him in its protective cushioning as he faced the whining, flashing bank of controls, his massive jaw jutting out over the sensor-pads, his deep dark eyes half closed in concentration.

Liz looked at the screen and saw the three wakes weaving a million-mile-wide pattern against the emptiness of the Quadrant. A great, jagged shard of energy hung momentarily around them.

"Now!" Maran bawled as it began to creep across the intervening reaches toward the *ES 110*.

And again the prison-ship danced madly into sable darkness, always away from the advancing onrush of force-fields. The drives faltered. Liz cried aloud, and Maran grated fresh commands. The ship seemed to hang still as the great cloud of forces neared it. Momentarily, the thrusting drive was inhibited.

"Emergency Phase!" Maran yelled. "Burn the engines out!"

The fabric of the vessel creaked.

"There's nowhere you can go!" Liz cried above the scream of the overworked drive and the complaints of a hundred systems.

Maran ignored Liz. His hands wove a fresh spell. Liz could wonder at his steadfast power. Without a tremor, he was working some fresh legerdemain that would take the ship beyond the reach of the cruisers.

The machine responded.

The *ES 110* howled, jangled, *screamed*!

"Kindly confirm latest instructions regarding expellees," said a Grade Two System.

"I advise an alteration of course," the Grade One robot said before Liz could begin to ask herself what the machines meant.

Maran again worked his strange chicanery and the machines were soothed. Nevertheless, the Grade One robot asked nervously:

"I take it, sir, that it is essential for the *ES 110* to continue the course indicated?" It waited. "If you say so, sir. Scanners report objective in view."

Liz looked at the operations screen.

There was a great blotch across the cosmos. She had seen it before. "No," she whispered, staring in disbelief. "Not now—not there!"

The ship gave a series of small, abrupt jerks.

Scanners ranged on the wake of the ship as Maran gave orders.

Dazed by the transition from the strange, spreading blotch that had so astounded her, she saw another incomprehensible sight.

In the eddying wake of the ship, scores of tiny objects tumbled end over end in a jerky, unsure jumble. She looked back at Maran. He was watching her.

"I should have sent you, too, Miss Deffant, but I could not." His hypnotic eyes held her. "Miss Deffant, have you ever met a person for the first time and had the most powerful intuition that you and that person were inextricably bound together?"

Liz knew the terrible irony of his words.

The grim-faced commander of the Enforcement Service cruiser saw the erratic movement of the prison-ship and wondered how long its drive could sustain the colossal pressures exerted on it.

"Anything from Rosario?" he asked.

"No, sir," said the young lieutenant. "He's in a coma."

"And we still don't know the situation out there."

"If it's Maran—"

"It's Maran."

"Then he's keeping us guessing, sir."

Though he did not allow it to show, the commander was worried. A humane and compassionate man, Commander Lientand had policed the cosmos for thirty years in a Service which he admired. He wished retirement had come earlier. He thought of what he might be called upon to do. Only once had he seen the ghastly, gobbeting power of the cruiser's main armament. It was a sight to forget. Somewhere within the depths of the cruiser, the golden pellets would be ready.

The ship on the huge screen suddenly leaped into a new framework of dimensions.

The field man fought silently to align the force-field which should have snuffed out the *ES 110*'s drive like a candle in a gale. Twice now, the prison-ship had eluded the blanketing concentration of energies.

"What's he trying?" the young lieutenant demanded. "He can't get away," he said, echoing Liz Deffant's words. "There's nowhere he can go!"

The field man frowned. There was a pattern about the

runaway ship's moves: one that made no sense at all. But a pattern nevertheless.

"Sir—" he began. He was interrupted by an excited report.

"Sighting of survival-cylinders, Commander!" a robot reported.

"Scores of them!" echoed the lieutenant. "It's the expellees—maybe the crew!"

"The ship could be breaking up!" another voice called.

Lientand rapped out orders. The three cruisers wheeled to claw in the scores of pods. It was a decision that had to be made instantly, for the cylinders were not designed for deep-space use. True, they had a certain capability of endurance, but a limited one. Rosario had been lucky.

"Maran's abandoned the ship!" yelled a crewman jubilantly. "We'll have him in a few minutes!'

The field man forgot his unformed yet uneasy moment. He was elated, like the other crewmen; the hunt was over. Lientand was smiling. There would be no need for the frightful holocaust of the sungun. They all watched the bobbing, weaving kaleidoscopic patterns in the prison-ship's wide, swirling wake. A successful action. The integrity of the Service had been preserved: never had they lost a ship. A particular delight was that the machines had failed: the robots had been unable to cope with the emergency.

"Sir!" yelled the field man, the first to realize that the *ES 110* had slipped away like some incorporeal manifestation faced with the dawn. He pointed to the screen. Thin tendrils of broken space showed where the prison-ship had been.

And then the reports came in.

The *ES 110* had jerked itself violently away from the space-time where the slowing cruisers and the oscillating survival-cylinders were making their rendezvous.

"I knew it made sense!" the field man yelled. "I didn't think anyone would use it—look, sir!" he shouted, pointing to a growing blotch on the screen. "That's where he was making for!"

Lientand cursed silently. Maran had used the pods to conceal his latest maneuver. Maran had outwitted him. "Engage main drive!" he called. "Emergency!" Seconds later, he added: "Range on the *ES 110*—main armament."

The young lieutenant gasped: "Sungun, sir!"

"He used the expellees as cover to delay us," said Lientand. "I should have guessed."

"But where can he go, sir?"

The field man pointed to the screen. "The Jansky Singularity."

The normal bodily processes seemed to be utterly irrelevant to what he had witnessed. Nevertheless, Buchanan found himself to be ravenously hungry. He was tired, too, he realized. He had not slept at all since the first sighting of the Jansky Singularity by the long-range scanners, and not much for days before that. Living seemed to be telescoped. Everything focused on the search.

Buchanan ate and wondered at his appetite. Was it that, by finding the *Altair Star*, by locating it, he was free of the tensions of the past three years? The thought disturbed him, for it led to other prospects. It led, for one thing, to thoughts of a time when he should have completed his mission. But that way led to despair. There was nothing for him now.

In a moment of clairvoyance, he understood that only a Liz Deffant could have brought him back into the range of normal human feeling. There would be no more of her kind. Not for Al Buchanan.

"Sleep," he told the cone-shaped pedestal.

"Yes, sir."

The bridge dimmed agreeably. A couch slid toward him, deeply foamed, utterly inviting.

"Six hours," he said. Six hours of deep, conditioned sleep, and then the eerie tunnel. He could wait that long. When he woke, he would take the station down into the depths and search out his ship.

Satisfied that he had almost come to the end of his quest, Buchanan settled to sleep. It was so nearly over. A bridge to that cocoon of forever. . . . It was possible. It had to be.

CHAPTER 13

Liz watched the operations screen as Maran indicated the *ES 110*'s course. Under his skilled direction, the scanners swam out through the uncertain dimensions, seeking their object. And they found it. Ripples of power surged in the blank regions. A network of bizarre serpentine coils spun across the cosmos. It all had a terrible familiarity. At the center of the whirling, coruscating mass was a sinking darkness.

"I have to lose the cruisers, you understand, Miss Deffant," Maran said. "In order to do so, I am taking this vessel briefly near the outer reaches of the Singularity. Our warp-shift wake disintegrates once we get near. It's a simple choice, you see, Miss Deffant. Maran on an obscure planet, or the culmination of a life's work."

Liz listened, a curious sense of relief drifting around her mind. She would be near Al. What a bitter coincidence of events, the take-over of the prison-ship and Al's haunted mission! As the *ES 110* shuddered under the strain of Maran's reckless urgings, Al would be somewhere at the peripheries of the Singularity trying to solve his own obsessive riddle. They were all to rendezvous at the raging efflorescence of the Jansky Singularity.

"The cruisers have slowed to take on the expellees," Maran said. "I used your idea, Miss Deffant."

"It was Commander Rosario's idea."

"Nevertheless, you were the decisive factor. I needed a small delay. I had to distract the cruisers so that they would think I had abandoned the ship."

"You think it's going to survive in *that*?"

They both looked at the coiled and majestic phenomenon that dominated the cosmos with its raging might.

Maran was serious to the point of portentousness:

"Miss Deffant, Maran must be free! There are things that only Maran can do. Never before has such a mind been brought to bear on the ultimate mystery." He put his hands to his large, gleaming skull. "Within this brain is a conjunction of powers and creative insight that is without parallel. Maran is the culmination of decades of research and dedicated experiment. And he is near—so near!—the realization of man's supreme vision!"

It was lunatic. Egocentric, megalomaniac, self-obsessed boasting that was almost ludicrous. Yet the sweat-streaked, huge face, the dark brooding eyes with their strange beauty, the very posture of that big body, all of these things, and then the resonant voice to give them meaning: Liz could understand how he had gained his proud followers.

"Give up," she said quietly. "Go to the Rim. Work there—plan but don't experiment. Your work will be recognized."

Maran spoke to her as if she were a child. "Maran on a bare rock, Miss Deffant, *Maran*? A stone hut and a musket? No, Miss Deffant. My unique genius needs the tools of this millennium."

"You could begin."

"Yes. Ten years, Miss Deffant. That's how long it would take. Ten years to mine the ores, refine the metals, make the primitive tools, begin to build the technological capacity for the equipment I must have." He looked at his big, white hands. "I am not a young man, Miss Deffant."

"They won't let you escape. They can't."

Maran sent scanners ranging far out into the uncertain dimensions. They brought back the cruisers' feral shapes. One of the hunted, Liz could also share the feelings of the hunters. She saw the three cruisers hanging starkly in the boiling incandescence of interdimensional haze. They left a huge triple parabola across the cosmos as they tried to sniff out the trail of the *ES 110.*

"Message beamed from Commander Lientand, sir," reported the Grade One robotic controller. It no longer attempted to offer advice to Maran. "Message warns of interdiction throughout the Quadrant. You are advised that this ship is now in an interdicted zone."

Liz felt a chill passing through her body. She knew the jargon of the Enforcement Service sufficiently well to understand what Commander Lientand was telling Maran.

"I think it would be as well to listen to the commander," said Maran. He gave orders. "It will be a close-run thing, Miss Deffant. Our warp-shift wake is breaking up, but they are closing."

He was worried, but his massive calmness had a reassuring effect on Liz. She realized helplessly that she was placing some kind of trust in this monstrous creature; his strangely haunting eyes had a warmth that did much to cancel out her fear of him. At the same time, she wanted him caught. Caught, not obliterated.

Commander Lientand was brief and precise: "Maran, you can't escape. I have a squadron of cruisers closing in. I have placed an interdiction on the Quadrant. It is my duty to apprehend you, but if I can't I am empowered to use my main armament to destroy the transport. I order you now to hold the *ES 110* in a normal condition of Phase and beam your present coordinates. You will be safe. Your treatment will be in accordance with Galactic Council Penal Code Regulations. You have my personal guarantee that all will be done to insure your well-being. Reply at once."

"He makes no mention of you," said Maran thoughtfully.

"It doesn't matter! Do as he says!"

"And you are not afraid for yourself," Maran said approvingly.

"I am! But it's over! The ship's not built to stand this kind of strain! Give it up!"

Low-grade systems complained bitterly. Maran swung the ship away on a new spiraling series of maneuvers, always toward the majestic menace of the Singularity. All over the great infragalactic ship, units were failing under the strain of the mad flight. Maran silenced the complaining machines, subordinating them, one by one, to his will. The fabric of the bridge shivered as it drifted near a small white star; Maran used its gusting radiation to sling the *ES 110* even more wildly toward the rotating blotch that was the Singularity.

"No reply, sir," reported the young lieutenant.

"Excuse me, Commander," the medical officer said. "There's something you should know."

Commander Lientand's thoughts were on the man who had seized an Enforcement Service vessel—arrogant, of lightning decision, adroit, a man of infinite resource. To destroy that mind was a cruel waste. Lientand's tired face remained grim.

"Well?"

"Rosario was conscious for a few moments, sir. He was asking about a girl."

"Girl? I see. One of the female expellees."

"No, sir. A passenger."

"Passenger! On the *ES 110*?"

"A female ecologist, sir. With New Settlements. She would have clearance, especially if she had friends at Center. Rosario was insistent, sir. Very distressed when we couldn't give him any assurances."

"She wasn't in a cylinder?"

"No, sir." The medical officer went on: "I'm guessing at this, but I think she's the one who gave him first aid. And then launched the two pods we picked up. Rosario in one, the other empty."

"So she stayed behind."

"Yes, sir."

Lientand watched the growth of the Jansky Singularity on the vast blue-pulsing screen. "She stayed with Maran."

"She is a Miss Elizabeth Deffant, single, sir. Rosario was rambling, but he remembered her name from the log."

"Did he say why she remained?"

"No, sir."

A girl, thought Lientand. It had not been easy to think of the holocaust swallowing up the *ES 110* and its bizarre commander; but he could have done it and lived with his conscience afterward. Lientand could only speculate helplessly on the impulse that had made the unknown Bureau girl send Rosario away to safety while she watched the empty survival-cylinder leave without her. Perhaps she had been afraid at the last moment. Perhaps the thought of the colossal storms of hyperspace spinning the tiny pod about was too much for her. He shook his head. Another thought struck him, but he dismissed it. The New Settlements people were highly-motivated and resourceful people: could it be, however remote the possibility, that she had stayed to confront Maran?

Maran! thought Lientand savagely. Maran had not answered his orders, not so much as replied with a single word. Maran knew the value of his position. There was everything to be gained by keeping his pursuers in doubt: by blanking off all communication with the cruisers, he could keep them guessing as to his intentions. The girl's presence was a bonus, a source of doubt and confusion.

"Sighting?" he asked.

"Nothing, sir," said his field man. "There's a lot of discontinuous action about the Singularity—we've lost his wake."

"Can you trace him?"

"With three sets of scanners, almost certainly, sir. We can do an integrated plot—"

"Do it. Sungun ranged on first sighting," he said to his young lieutenant. "Shoot on my order."

"Sir! The girl—"

Lientand silenced the opposition. Bleakly he said: "I won't take my ships into *that*." He pointed to the raging fury of the Singularity. "And I won't risk losing Maran."

"But there is the girl, sir," the medical officer insisted. Tight-lipped, he faced Lientand's drawn face. "She saved Rosario."

Lientand turned away. "She would forgive me."

Buchanan had been asleep for more than five hours when the *ES 110* registered its presence in the locality of the Jansky Singularity. There was a subdued metallic discussion and then, eventually, a decision. The couch began to heave gently. Impulses were directed through nerve-centers. Tiny alerts jangled, speaking of an emergency.

"Report," said Buchanan, yawning in spite of the sharp tingling of nerve-ends. The deep uninterrupted sleep had restored him, but it still invested his tissues.

"This system has readings of approach of a Galactic Service vessel, sir. Designation: Enforcement Service vessel One-Hundred class."

"A transport."

"Yes, sir. On routine voyage to the Rim. Crew of six, accommodation for—"

"About a hundred expellees."

"Modified for control-monitoring of not more than eighty expellees," the robot corrected.

Buchanan was not even mildly irritated. He remembered the earlier message. "Show."

"Yes, sir."

Scanners ranged and Buchanan saw the transport. Its warp-shift scattered wide showers of broken molecules.

"It's the *ES 110*!"

"Yes, sir."

Buchanan realized that the deep sleep had drugged his senses. He punched commands and allowed sensor-pads to slide into his palms. Information roared into his mind. He lost his sleepy, relaxed look. The craggy features became sharper, the eyes narrowed; his wiry body became taut with suppressed muscular energy.

"You let me sleep!" he exploded after a minute. "While Red Alerts go out from three cruisers—when there's a hijacked prison-ship heading for us!"

"Your instructions, Commander, were that you be left to sleep. There are no standing orders overriding your instructions. This system did take it upon itself to awaken you when your sleep-requirement quotient was effectively satisfied."

Buchanan snorted and then contained his useless anger. He scanned the bulky transport as it soared around the edges of a decaying white dwarf star. Its engines pushed space and clouds of interstellar dust aside. A blast of solar wind obscured its drive: on the screen, the wake showed as an uneven tidal wave.

"What in the name of God is it doing?" Buchanan expostulated. "Don't they know what the Singularity can do? Beam direct—warn the ship!"

"Automatic signals have been beamed for the past nineteen minutes and eight seconds, sir. There has been no acknowledgment. Damage is reported by our scanners. The *ES 110* is engaged in a series of dangerous maneuvers. It is approaching the critical area of the discontinuities zone. Power readings from the *ES 110* indicate an insufficient level for survival should condition of starquake begin."

"Put me on to its commander!"

"Yes, sir."

Buchanan felt the rush of urgency as a message came strongly through his palms. A high-powered signal on the Enforcement Service Red Alert beamers was on its way. As Buchanan waited, a laconic system reported that the Singularity was again heaving its coils in a slow, massive pattern.

Then the operations screen filled with an image of the cruiser squadron's commander. Buchanan recognized the features of Commander Lientand. He waited for the message to come winging through the unreal dimensions. A vague but profound premonition began to trouble him; he had been alone with his haunted memories, and now the busy turbulent life of the Galaxy was seeking him out. His concern had been with the dead—with the ghosts who thronged his mind; and here was Lientand and an errant transport. Buchanan bit his lip. He wanted no part of the transport's problems. Nor Lientand's.

Yet the *ES 110* was even now blasting furiously toward the Singularity.

"Commander Buchanan," said the laconic system. "Renewed activity suggestive of starquake—"

"Wait!"

Lientand was speaking, not entirely clearly, but clearly enough to be understood: "I am Commander Lientand. My ship is an Enforcement Service cruiser. I have under my command two more cruisers. My assignment is to capture the Enforcement Service transport *ES 110*. It is in the hands of the criminal Maran—"

"Maran!" Buchanan could not help calling. "*Maran*?"

Lientand could not hear him, but he must have known the impression his words would create. "I repeat, the *ES 110* is in the hands of the criminal Maran. We have located the ship and attempted to inhibit its drives, so far without success. Maran has taken the *ES 110* into the vicinity of the Jansky Singularity, where his warp-shift wake may be concealed. It may be impossible for my cruisers to arrest the ship, in which case I shall destroy it. The Quadrant is now an interdicted zone. All ships receiving this message must leave the Quadrant immediately."

Buchanan knew the reason for the *ES 110*'s apparently suicidal maneuvers. Maran would try anything to evade the pursuing Enforcement Service vessels. But why had he chosen *now* to make his escape bid?

"Have you established reciprocal contact with the *ES 110*?" he snapped to the Grade One robot.

"Not yet, sir."

"Beam to the cruiser—message received and understood! Tell Commander Lientand Maran's here. And tell him his ship's damaged!"

"Of course, sir."

He looked at the big screen as robotic systems simulated the transport's wild course. Suddenly a gobbeting, snaking coil flooded the screen, engulfing the prison-ship.

"No!" whispered Buchanan.

"I'm afraid so, sir," said the metallic voice sympathetically. "It was always a possibility, sir."

Maran had gambled with his life. This time, he had lost. Nothing could help the *ES 110*. Nevertheless, even a

Maran deserved a warning. Buchanan thought of the other condemned men and women aboard the ship. And the crew.

Abruptly he called: "Jansky Station to *ES 110*! This is Buchanan, Jansky Singularity Experimental Station—calling *ES 110*! Utmost danger exists—turn away at once—burn the drives out if you have to—but turn away from the Singularity! Starquake conditions exist—turn away now!"

The station's powerful beamers began to reach out across the gulfs and through the serpentine coils of the Singularity. Surely Maran would try to save himself?

"*ES 110*—I repeat, starquake conditions exist! If you turn away now and use maximum emergency power you may pull away—call the cruisers and ask for combined fields to help you!"

Buchanan could not bring himself to address Maran directly. But there was the rest of the *ES 110*'s complement—perhaps the crew could reason with Maran. Maybe they could persuade him to try to save himself and the future of his stupendous, visionary schemes.

There was nothing he could do now but report to Lientand. Quietly he spoke into the beamer channel: "This is Buchanan at the Jansky Singularity Station. I have Commander Lientand's message. The *ES 110* is approaching the rim of the Jansky Singularity. Violent starquake conditions exist. I am doubtful of the ability of the *ES 110* to survive for many minutes. Maran does not respond to my warnings. It is my opinion that the *ES 110* was taken to the Singularity deliberately. Have you any instructions for me?"

Buchanan saw the transport clearly as it blasted across a glowing pit of incandescent radiation. There was a decayed air about it—bits of fittings trailed away; the drive jerked the ship about spasmodically; an unidentifiable section broke away from the stern and sank into the haze of the discontinuities. Another ship would join the silent, time-lost fleet.

The Jansky Singularity was claiming another ghost-ship.

CHAPTER 14

The big battle-screen pulsed blue and then filled with the great efflorescence of the Singularity. Scanners darted about, leaving gossamer trails and bringing back only unidentifiable, almost unfathomable readings. Lientand thought of the New Settlements Bureau girl. He wondered what she must be going through now, as the *ES 110* plunged into the Singularity's fields.

"There!" yelled the field man suddenly.

On the screen, the *ES 110* appeared. It hung like a broken moth against the frightful attraction of the raging depths. There could be no doubt about it. It was the ship. The superb scanners had been able to locate the ringing shards of its broken warp-shift, in spite of Maran's maneuvers.

Lientand tensed, face gray with grim pity. He would do it himself, his hand releasing the gobbeting fury that would tear across space with the force of a supernova and expunge the lives of the two human beings aboard the *ES 110*.

"She'll forgive me," he whispered to himself.

The sensor-pad in his palm demanded assent. The deadly golden pellet waited to be ejected from the long snout of the cruiser. Warning sirens shrieked to the other cruisers: beware!

Lientand breathed in deeply, the order rising to his lips.

"Sir!" shouted the young lieutenant.

Lientand almost said the word, almost released the sunburst, almost wiped out the two lives. But he stopped.

"Well?" he grated, bile in his mouth.

"Beam from Buchanan, sir!"

"Buchanan?"

The strain of the terrible seconds had left a mark. Then Lientand remembered. Buchanan. A wreck—not many years ago. And, recently, something else—

"The Jansky Station, sir! The new crewed research beacon—Buchanan at the Singularity!"

"Yes." He remembered it now. It had seemed a strange appointment to him. Buchanan had survived a ghastly wreck, and he had been appointed to this experimental ship. "Go on."

"We got a repeat beam—from a robot beacon. There's a lot of distortion from the *ES 110*, sir. It's heading into the Singularity—and Buchanan says the Singularity's brewing up for starquake!"

"He'd have hoped to lose us," said Lientand slowly. "Now he's lost. And the girl." He pushed the sensor-pad away. "Keep ranging. Gunners at action stations."

He watched but they did not see the doomed ship again. All aboard the cruiser could imagine the progress of the transport as it was swept nearer and nearer the rotating, blurred ragged hole where Buchanan's tiny station hung.

"Buchanan asked for instructions, sir," said the young lieutenant.

"I'll talk to him," said the tired man.

Buchanan saw that the ship was blind, almost helpless. Its drive left a churning, twisting shape briefly among the tongues lapping out from the Singularity. Tendrils of power snaked out from the rotating coruscation and flung it about. Buchanan sensed as a physical thing the jerking, rushing movement of the *ES 110*. He remembered another ship that had left him reeling with vertigo as it danced and plunged in the grip of starquake until it was at the edge of the great maw of the Singularity.

Inevitably the *ES 110* must join that strange fleet, that time-lost collection of silent ships. It would be a doubly bizarre end for the expellees in their coma-cells, for they would be embalmed in the cocoon of foreverness without ever waking to their danger.

Buchanan located the cruiser squadron. They held off, coasting well beyond the Singularity's lapping tongues. They had chased the hijacked ship until it was forced against the swirling fields of the Singularity. Their task was over. Inside the transport, Maran and those that survived would realize it.

Already they must know that it was too late to surrender. When Buchanan had called to Maran, there was only the remotest of possibilities of saving the ship. Only a freak combination of fields, such as that which had saved him three years before, would enable the prison-ship to loosen the grip of the serpentine coils. The ship's failing engines would not provide shields for long against the strange vortices.

It was a doomed, dying ship.

Buchanan watched its inelegant shape as the Singularity reached out. He could sense the tumult within the Singularity through the pads in his hands. Starquake was imminent, might even now be mangling space and time. The black hole would open, the ship would lurch through—

"Starquake confirmed, sir," a robot voice informed him.

Buchanan spoke again to the cruiser commander: "I ask again, have you any instructions for me, Commander Lientand? I have your message regarding Maran and the *ES 110*. This is Buchanan at the Jansky Singularity Station. I have your message. I have just seen the *ES 110* begin to enter the Singularity. Starquake condition is confirmed. The *ES 110* is going, Commander. Starquake emissions have the ship. No ship can hold against these conditions. I repeat, have you any instructions for me?"

Not that there's anything I can do, thought Buchanan.

"Buchanan, Jansky Station," he called again. "The *ES 110*'s going."

Impelled by a macabre curiosity, he moved the station closer and closer to the doomed transport. The little station edged among increasingly powerful surgings as the effects of starquake split the dimensions. And then Buchanan saw the twisting ship clearly.

Inside it, was Maran fighting for his life? Was he trying some desperate expedient in a vain effort to hold back the blackness at the Singularity's core?

He could not succeed. The drive was visibly failing. Buchanan watched its jagged, fading wake. Often the ship was totally obscured by the boiling waves of the Singularity's emissions. What remained of power in the *ES 110* was a weak, splintered thrust. Nothing could save Maran. There was no chance that the robotic systems could hurl a part of the ship clear of the Singularity, for the engines were dying.

The little station slid nearer, a greased nut in the bizarre serpentine coils. Buchanan saw the details of the prison-ship's last plummeting flight. Great chunks of the ship fell away. A complete engine pod burst into a nuclear holocaust, to be instantly extinguished by the weird emissions from the black hole. Snuffed out, the engine's debris at once drifted into the core.

Buchanan was fascinated and horrified by the big infragalactic ship's end. It was so like the last careering plunge of the *Altair Star*. Again, an overwhelming freak of nature was gobbling a minuscule and frail victim. Struggle as it might, the ship could do nothing.

By the time the cruiser commander acknowledged Buchanan's reports, the *ES 110* was a wreck. The Singularity's roaring fields almost wiped out the powerfully-beamed message, but enough of it came through. Buchanan listened as he saw the prison-ship begin to fall apart.

". . . Buchanan at . . . cruiser. . . . Your message received. . . . agreed, Buchanan, there can be no hope. . . . My field man's readings . . . starquake emissions. . . ." Lientand's voice crackled. And there was a long break, so that Buchanan's attention was diverted to the screen. But Lientand's voice, as well as his image, came through clearly for the latter part of his message, the part that burned into Buchanan's mind like white fire: "Especially regret the loss of the courageous woman passenger. She enabled Commander Rosario to escape just before Maran released the surviving expellees. If you can do anything to get a message to her, please do so, Buchanan. Tell her Commander Rosario is safe. And the rest of the expellees were picked up unharmed. It's largely through her efforts that Maran was traced. I know there is nothing any of us can do to help her, but let her know at least that we are all in her debt. My instructions, Buchanan, are that you should tell Elizabeth Deffant that—"

It was all Buchanan heard, for though Lientand's voice went on the words would not register. Buchanan saw the gray face, the long jaw, the lean upright body. The beam came from a cruiser hovering beyond the Singularity's peripheries, and it showed the commander's image: his face, with the lips moving and words coming out slowly, a face gray with fatigue and with lines of age etched deeper by mental torment. The man was suffering, Buchanan recognized. And he was ordering him, Buchanan, to get a message to—

". . . Deffant?" he whispered. "You said 'Elizabeth Deffant'?"

The shape of the commander vanished as the processes that made up the seismic monstrosity of starquake struck out and splayed the dimensions adrift. Buchanan was unable to respond.

"He said—" and moments passed as Buchanan, slit-eyed, jaws clenched, his thin face white, repeated the commander's message. "He said—aboard the *ES 110*—Liz?"

Thoughts spun wildly about his tormented mind. *Liz*? Liz Deffant on the prison-ship? *Why*?

It was inconceivable. Enforcement Service ships didn't carry passengers. Their function was to take expellees to newfound star-systems. Liz had been on her way to her home planet, to Messier 16, not to the Rim of the Galaxy!

Buchanan sweated coldly as seconds passed. Futile questions rang around his mind. Worse answers followed. And he would not admit that he had heard Lientand's words.

"No," said Buchanan.

It had been an effect of starquake distortion. That, and his own guilt feelings. He had imagined Lientand's message. He had invented the commander's mention of an Elizabeth Deffant because his loneliness had worked on his mind to such an extent that he had needed to hear someone mention her.

"Ravings—hallucinations," Buchanan decided.

Lientand hadn't said anything about a woman passenger who saved commanders. Especially Lientand hadn't said a word about a Liz Deffant who was nowhere near the Singularity—who was making for her home planet in a fit of righteous indignation at being cast off like an old shoe!

Buchanan blinked. *Wrong*.

"He said 'Elizabeth Deffant.'" And Buchanan reached for the writhing sensor-pads. "He did," he repeated slowly.

He called for information with a deadly calm.

"Data on *ES 110*!" he ordered. "Possibility of a woman passenger named Elizabeth Deffant, employee of New Settlements Bureau, shipping out to Messier 16, being aboard *ES 110*. Soonest."

The Grade One robot was efficient. The answer came within a second: "This ship's systems have no data on a woman named Deffant, but it's a distinct possibility that Commander Lientand is right. As a Galactic Service employee, she would be entitled to travel on all Service ships with vacant accommodation. Regulations allow for it, sir, but not many take advantage of the facility. It's unusual, sir, not unheard of."

"She was going to Messier 16!"

"All the more likely, then, sir," the machine pointed out, helpfully smashing down Buchanan's hopes. "The *ES 110* was scheduled to pass near enough for the regular shuttle to intercept, sir." It paused. "I have a full recording of Commander Lientand's message, sir."

"I expect you have."

"I thought you were denying the validity of the commander's message, sir. It's quite clear. A Miss Deffant is aboard the *ES 110*."

Not Liz! And, with a silent plea, Buchanan accepted it. Liz Deffant was drifting away, silently spinning into the eerie depths of the Jansky Singularity. He groaned aloud. It was too macabre a coincidence, too sick a triumph of a vengeful fate. The inconceivable was happening as he watched. Liz was joining the ghost-fleet.

Maran fought the ship even as it died.

He worked in a determined frenzy, shearing off defunct systems, abandoning an engine that threatened to rip the vessel apart, calling on remote and rarely-used emergency circuits to add their power to the weak thrust of decaying engines. It could never be enough, Liz knew. The Singularity had them. The ship was wrenched about in short, bone-shaking surges. The fabric of the *ES 110* was buckling. Writhing tendrils of alien energies threaded through submicroscopic orifices.

The Singularity was claiming the ship. And the *ES 110* could do nothing. High-grade systems had ceased to clamor for relief. Liz found it especially frightening that no more warnings came from the robots.

They recognized the impossibility of their task.

Liz cried out in true fear as a shock wave hit the ship.

Maran's huge face streamed with sweat. He too was afraid, but for him the physical fear of personal extinction was nothing; Liz sensed his obsessive agony. He was terrified that he would never complete his ten-million year search for the moment of transition of beast to man, never range the inner depths and bring out, dripping, the gem of information that was buried somewhere beneath the overlay of a half-million lifetimes.

Liz Deffant stared, unable to restrain a choking gasp of awe at his struggle. There was a primeval force loose on the bridge: Maran, that strange elemental being that was so remote from a humanity he sought to explain, was trying to wrest the ship out of the Singularity's grip. And it was no use.

A penumbra of black light flooded the bridge. The bright-painted walls buckled. And still Maran stood at the console. Even though the ship was breaking up about him, Maran held the machines to his purpose.

In a tormented delirium, Buchanan called for every particle of energy the station could exert. He drove the small vessel through the writhing, serpentine coils with the fury of desperation. The ship spun wildly, gripped on a writhing hump of uncanny forces, and eased itself toward the boiling fields where the *ES 110* hung. Skills acquired in years of infragalactic flight among the reefs of hyperspace enabled him to squeeze the Jansky Station nearer and nearer the fraying transport. *Liz*! his mind was yelling, but he said nothing. Not until a rumble of metallic discontent came from the machines.

He silenced it bitterly: "Get nearer the *ES 110*!"

"Sir, starquake emission reports show as yet uncharted emissions. The transport is in a configuration of maximum danger!"

"All engines at ultimate power! Any risk—get near that ship!"

Buchanan watched the vessel shredding. A decaying area of black light hung around the drive housing. There was little to show that its remaining engines still functioned; a jagged scar was all that remained of one engine pod. The *ES 110* trembled and fluttered like a wounded insect, spinning on its axis and describing a powerless course within the serpentine coils that were drawing it into the vortex.

It was the *Altair Star* all over again, but this time it was so much worse. Buchanan could feel Kochan's corrosive grief as if it were his own. Liz, joining the silent long-gone who might not be dead! Not a company of expellees —not Enforcement Service crewmen who would have known the risks of their job—not impersonal strangers one could feel a real but distant pity for: it was Liz Deffant who was being taken into the black pit. And Maran.

Buchanan tried again to gain contact with the doomed ship.

"Buchanan at the Jansky Station calling Maran!"

Before he had known that Liz was aboard the *ES 110*

he had not been able to use Maran's name. Not directly. Now, he would do anything.

"Maran!" Even though it was hopeless, he tried. "Maran, this is Buchanan! I'm trying to get near you! This is a special research ship—I'll try to reach you!"

But what could he do then? Within the station he was safe—it had weathered the uncertainties of the Singularity even when starquake had occurred to multiply its hazards. But how could he reach the *ES 110*? How could he or anyone from the ship cross the wild and bizarre regions?

Buchanan turned to the machines. Set up the possibilities, he ordered. Soon, the Grade One robot answered.

Impossible, came the reply. Impossible to build any kind of space-raft that would be capable of withstanding the stresses of the Singularity.

He ordered a fresh analysis, given the wildest freaks of chance.

It responded glumly.

Given luck, admitted the robotic controller, a gap *might* be found through which a small fragment of the *ES 110* could be ejected into a safer framework of dimensions, perhaps even to the cruisers. But there had to be massive initial thrust. It demonstrated a series of possibilities, and Buchanan's hopes died.

With luck—with the most freakish luck, the right combination of energy fields and the abrupt force of the ship's engines, some kind of life-raft could be blasted clear of the Singularity.

Buchanan scanned estimates, forecasts, projections.

"Well?" he asked, knowing the answer.

No, the Grade One robot said judicially, *not in the case of the ES 110*. Its power-levels were too low. Absurdly low.

The small miracle of the *Altair Star* would not be repeated.

There would be not even one survivor.

Without hope, Buchanan would not give up.

"Maran! Put the woman Deffant in a life-raft!" he yelled into the blankness before him. "Yourself too—I swear I'll try to save you! The robots say it can't be done, but maybe I can get some kind of field rigged up—try, Maran! Get a life-raft made. For you—and the woman!"

The fatigue showed in Maran's face. His eyes were opaque, their hypnotic beauty dimmed. Through the sound of metal shrieking, force-screens jangling appallingly, and distant systems advising that they were defunct, Liz could hear his grated orders. He would not surrender to the inevitable. The man was invested with a rage to survive, and Liz was freshly amazed at the supremacy of his vision. He played the machines as if they were delicate music, and while they gradually lapsed into quiescence he soothed them, wringing each last note of power as they died. When she recalled how she had tried to shoot him with the ponderous, archaic weapon, Liz could have wept. She felt no more bitter anger at Maran.

It was a betrayal of her regard for the young man she had known for such a short time; it was a betrayal, too, of all her instincts and training; yet she could not hate Maran, either for what he had done so horribly to his deluded followers, or for the murder of the Enforcement Service personnel. There was a pitiable quality in his desperation. And she pitied him.

Al Buchanan's voice seemed part of the nightmare at first.

". . . I swear I'll try to save you! The robots say it can't be done, but maybe I can get some kind of field rigged up —Try, Maran!" His voice rang through the black-flooding bridge. "Get a life-raft made. For you—and the woman!"

Liz realized that she had not thought of the station as a means of help. So bewildered had she been that she had thought of Al as nearby but not within possible reach. And this was his voice calling with a contained desperation to Maran! And to a woman.

Did he know she was on the ship?

"I repeat—get the woman Deffant and yourself into a life-raft!"

Liz cried out in pain, relief, abandoned joy, frustrated happiness.

Maran reacted instantly. "Reciprocal contact! Get me this Buchanan!"

Failing systems hoarsely assured him that they would try. He wove his big white hands over the console and armored servitors appeared. Suddenly the bridge was alive with movement, where before it had seemed a dying organism.

"Miss Deffant! This station—you know it?"

Liz tried to refuse the information. Al was trying to reach her, but Maran was a deadly threat to the hundreds who might be involved in his next series of grotesque experiments, to thousands who might follow them. But she could not. She had reached the end of her ability to resist the urge to live.

Al was the voice of promised life.

She could not deny the promise. And she could not speak.

Intently, Maran said to her: "I thought I should never say this to another person, Miss Deffant, but I must do so. Do not think I talk to you in this way because I am afraid to die—I am not. I am talking to you as an equal—and for the first time to any man or woman!—because I care that you understand. I do care that you have the facts. That you are able to judge for yourself why I have to survive now—that I have to reach this man Buchanan who means something to you. I must have your confidence and his help, and this is why. Listen."

And, strangely in the midst of preparations, clamorings, the noises of the disintegrating ship and the robots' exchanges, Liz listened with the deepest attention.

"I know," said Maran, "that there are farsighted and dedicated men and women in positions of authority who would help me. They know the value of my work and they know that I am the only man who can do it. They know Maran is unique. They admit that there should be agencies of change in the Galaxy if man is to venture beyond it. Before he can go farther out to the ends of the Universe, he must first learn to explore himself. Miss Deffant, the key to all knowledge is in here!"

Maran rested his hands on his sweating head. He had the look of a visionary priest who is ready to make a prophecy.

"There are also the inhibitors who cannot yet see that what we have done in this Galaxy is only a beginning. They cannot yet see that the Galaxy is only the microcosm. And it is these malignant creatures—the men of no vision —who have decreed that Maran must live like an ape on a rock! They would send this brain, this mind, this soul, to the Rim of the Galaxy in company with a cargo of poor lost psychopaths, and condemn it to extinction." He paused, and Liz could feel with him the sense of time passing, of visions swimming into the void unrealized, the waste, the venomous opposition of the small-minded, the soaring fantasy of his mind. "In the long-term, it is the great, creative minds that win, Miss Deffant. Always, there is more vitality in creation than in the negation of the human spirit. But in the short-term, it is the inhibitors who win. They have the authority to suppress the individual genius of a particular man. They can delay the passage of the human spirit for a measurable time—for a life-span, perhaps more. And, certainly, they can deny a Maran. They can send Maran to a bleak planet where the predators and the harsh climate make bare existence a heavy and unending battle. But Maran would begin now, Miss Deffant! Maran would change the whole direction of the human race! Maran knows where the search begins to unleash the infinitely gigantic genius of the human race! Maran can unlock the deepest wells of the human spirit!"

And once more Liz Deffant saw the uncanny effects on Maran of the repetition of his name. *Maran.* The word boomed out in his rolling bass voice with the effect of a drumbeat. When he spoke of himself, his eyes lost their cloudiness. They shone clear, like beacons. His face lost its flat planes and swelled like a great orb. His body cowered in the gloom of the shredding vessel, and among the robots which were his acolytes, he looked like a deity. "Maran can show you as well, Miss Deffant, that the power of the human spirit can surmount even the boundaries of time!"

She did not know what he meant, and cared less. He no longer frightened her. His presence inspired her with a feeling of religious awe, and she believed that he was what he said, a man of a unique mold, one who could wrench the veils from the ultimate mysteries and discover the secret of man's enigmatic rise from the beast.

"The station, Miss Deffant?"

"It's a new, experimental device," she answered. "Crewed by one man. Designed for observation of the Singularity. It has the capability to withstand all recorded emissions. It can operate at will within the peripheries of the Singularity, or so its engineers claim."

"Buchanan?"

"My fiancée. My former fiancée."

Maran nodded, ponderous head bending in sympathy. "He has a regard for you."

"I believe so."

"And you for him?"

"Does it matter?"

"It might, Miss Deffant."

"Yes."

"A strange meeting."

Liz felt hollow. Too many emotions had raged within her. She needed rest. Deep oblivion. She had seen two men whose every thought had centered on a single, obsessive vision. First Buchanan, now Maran. They had bled her of energy. She was as passive as the dead leaves she and Buchanan had once kicked away as they ran through an autumn wood when the sun flickered through branches full of yellow and gold.

"Miss Deffant, I have the feeling that we were preordained to meet. You and I. Buchanan and yourself. Buchanan and I. I shall try to make the meeting possible."

He redoubled his efforts at the console. All about the ship, failing robots answered his summons. Low-grade servitors finished the task of building a make-shift raft. Higher-grade systems shored up failing screens with the remnants of their power-sources. The entire vessel willingly gave up its last resource to insure that the god of the machines received his due. And, at last, there was reciprocal contact with the Jansky Singularity Station.

Liz heard a flat metallic voice announce the presence of the station and the man she had loved: "Jansky Singularity Station closing. Two scanners have visual contact."

"Near," said Maran.

"Engines operating at four percent efficiency. No reserve. Estimated drive capability at minimum levels, seven minutes at this utilization rate."

"Seven minutes," said Maran. "I hope your Buchanan is a man of resource."

Liz realized that she was too tired, too shocked, too used, to answer. She had no response to offer, none at all.

"This ship is in an immeasurable gravitational and electromagnetic conjunction of forces," said the robotic controller. "Increasing in complexity and magnitude. Source is the Jansky Singularity."

"This system can maintain a vocal contact with Commander Buchanan at the Jansky experimental station," announced another robot system.

Liz tensed.

"Let me speak to him," said Maran.

And Buchanan's craggy features began to filter through the appalling vortices. Liz Deffant saw the man who had gone to search out the ghosts of the *Altair Star*.

CHAPTER 15

Buchanan followed the twisting course of the *ES 110* as the coils of starquake held it. The Singularity's motions were those of a rapacious predator; it would not give up its prey now. The *ES 110* was to be ingested.

"Commander Buchanan, I have direct contact with an officer called Maran, but I should warn you, sir, that my colleague aboard the *ES 110* has information that this officer is also an expellee. In addition—"

"Direct—get me Maran!"

And Buchanan glimpsed the shadowy outline of a broad, heavy-featured face with straining eyes, a familiar face: Maran. But Buchanan was peering around the shadowy image of the man; he tried to make out the figures that moved like ponderous wraiths behind him. Machines! No sign of the slim shape of the woman who had almost exorcised the demons that rode his spirit. Where was Liz?

Maran was speaking. Across the broken dimensions, the words came haltingly: ". . . life-raft with all possible power-units . . . any way of using your screens . . ." And though much was lost, Buchanan knew that Maran was appealing for assistance. ". . . a woman passenger named Elizabeth Deffant, Buchanan!" Buchanan heard, almost clearly. What was Maran saying?

That Liz was safe? Or that she had already succumbed to the smashing fury of starquake?

For Buchanan there was an eternity of agonized waiting as the station's scanners lost contact with the decaying prison-ship. Momentarily, the robots picked it up again. End over end the great infragalactic ship tumbled, strewing wreckage in a shower of nameless fragments. And then the sensor-pads informed Buchanan that he could again speak to Maran.

"The Singularity's throwing out starquake. Maran, I'll try to get near. Get into the life-raft and lay the bridge open—keep to the ship as long as it has some power! If you and the woman get into the raft, I'll try to lock it into my screens. I say again, hold to the ship for as long as you can! It will give the life-raft some protection! And get the woman into the life-raft! Use deep-space armor—all you can carry!"

The three huge engines of the station screamed as the massive drive built to a crescendo. Incomprehensible energies sprang outward as starquake raged. The cruisers ran from the menace of the serpentine coils, seeking calmer dimensions. Buchanan called again to the lost ship, but there was no answer. *Liz!* he called silently.

"Maran, Maran!" he called. "No contact! Get the woman Deffant into a life-raft!"

"Beam from the *ES 110*," cut in the calm voice of the Grade One robot. "Commander, the expellee who seems also to be an Enforcement Service officer has impressed my colleague aboard the *ES 110* with the urgency of the situation. He has a proposal which, I am bound to say—"

"Direct!" snarled Buchanan. "Direct to Maran!"

So Maran was devising some scheme for his own self-preservation. Buchanan was past caring how much a danger the escaped man might be: he had one overwhelming concern. Against the safety of Liz Deffant, nothing mattered, nothing had ever mattered, not the futile quest for the *Altair Star*, not all those lost passengers and crew; and certainly not the grotesque personality of a Maran!

The broad, sweating face swam into view. A pulsing of sensor-pads told Buchanan that Maran could see him, in turn. Warnings irradiated his nerve-endings; Maran was trying to cut into the command-systems of the station.

". . . the only way," Maran was saying to him. "I know from your high-grade systems that your ship is under your control. It gives me a chance, Buchanan," he said urgently. "This vessel has power for only a few minutes! Give me direct access to your ship's memory-banks—allow me to take over its decision-making procedures! I could do it myself, given time, but there is no time! I have Miss Deffant's welfare to consider, Buchanan! I know it's important to you—do as I say, Buchanan, and I might . . ."

And again, to leave Buchanan writhing with agonized impatience, the coils of the Singularity blotted out all beamer channels.

"Liz!" he yelled, knowing she could not hear. But she

was safe—*safe*! he thought wildly, safe if Maran's word could be trusted, safe for a few minutes, and then the lunging descent into nothingness! Maran knew the connection between Liz and himself—she must have told him. And Maran would know that he would try any course of action, no matter how dangerous or traitorous, so long as there was the faintest of hopes that she could be pulled back from the black center of the Singularity and its promise of eternal silence, unending night.

The machines were uneasy. The Grade One robot voiced their doubts: "I view these proceedings and proposals with alarm," it began. "My colleague aboard the *ES 110* suggests that the criminal Enforcement officer Maran be given free access to the readings so far accumulated at the Singularity. More, it suggests that Maran is a suitable person to control other functions of this ship now delegated to yourself, sir!"

Buchanan collected his scattered thoughts. His craggy face was aflame with rage as he yelled at the pedestal which housed the robot: "No comments, no suggestions, no interference! Never!"

Even as he yelled, he realized how he had come to treat the machines as somehow personalized.

". . . sir," the machine responded, in its flat metallic voice.

"Agreed," Buchanan said across the gulfs that separated him from the *ES 110*. "Anything, Maran."

He knew he was conniving at the release of a man condemned by the Galactic Council as the greatest threat to mankind since the madness of the early Confederation days. If Maran could reach the station, he could hold it for a year.

But what was the alternative?

Refuse to help him, and Liz Deffant would join the eerie unlife of the time-lost tunnel. She would be beyond recall. Maran might do more and worse damage than he had done already; but if Maran the cyberneticist believed that he could work some kind of miracle among the robots' resources, then it must be so. There was no time for dispute.

Buchanan relinquished the sensor-pads as the first authoritative, insidious commands seeped into the station. Soothing, elegant instructions had the sensors-pads writhing in expectant ecstasy. Buchanan looked down at the console and knew that he was giving up all he had lived by during his years of Galactic Service, as well as his quest for the *Altair Star*. And nothing mattered, none of it.

The robotic controller raised no more objections. It became Maran's slave as soon as it picked up his wheedling, harsh, irresistible commands. Buchanan monitored the sequences with a growing wonder.

Maran called on the powerful, sophisticated memory-banks to give every last detail of the observed data associated with the Singularity. He demanded—and received—readings of which Buchanan knew nothing. The robots recognized the touch of the master-cyberneticist as Maran's personality infected the controlling devices of the station.

Maran heard the machines offhandedly mention the theories which they had decided were impossible, and his response was instantaneous.

"Steady-state?" he demanded.

"It's only a theory," Buchanan was driven to interrupt. "I think there might be—"

"Report on screen strengths necessary to stabilize the station in steady-state conditions," Maran rapped.

"Such hypotheses are interesting as speculations," the Grade One robot told Maran pedantically. "However, they must be regarded only as probably unlikely interpretations of conflicting data. In the absence of systematic recordings—"

Maran cut in abruptly: "Devise a warp capable of containing such a steady-state!"

Buchanan tensed. The two ships were close now, the sickening descent temporarily arrested as a flurry of vortices blustered against one another and created a pocket of relative calm. The unlikely elements were giving the *ES 110* a breathing-space. And Maran was using it to try to convince the robots that they should attempt the impossible.

He was trying to save the *ES 110* as, three years before, Buchanan had tried to save the *Altair Star*. The difference was that Maran was using his unique abilities to change the direction of the machines' conclusions.

Buchanan had attempted to wreck the robots; Maran made them his puppets.

Buchanan watched as the prison-ship lost a great chunk of its lower decks. Fragments of equipment, stores, engines, and unidentifiable debris hung in the grip of the Singularity's fields.

"This system is not designed to measure the impossible,

nor to create a technology capable of withstanding the impossible," the machine answered primly.

Buchanan watched the last struggles of the *ES 110.* Surely it was lost now? He followed the flow of information that was streaming across the impassable gap between the two ships.

Maran checked and rechecked the data. Especially he wanted the few available readings which the machines would admit to concerning the eerie tunnel where the ghost-fleet hung in the eddying fields of white-gold translucence.

"This system suggests that Commander Maran regard himself as defunct," the Grade One system announced. "Estimated power-reserves of the *ES 110* now give three minutes' duration capability."

"Warp," Maran said, more to himself than to the machines.

"Impossible, sir," the robot answered.

Buchanan thought sickly of Liz Deffant, who would be waiting to hear the cold information that would tell her of the failure of the *ES 110*'s last power-reserves. And yet he could not accept that she would be lost. Not while Maran fought the chilling logic of the robots.

Buchanan saw the man's face. Straining every nerve, he was concentrating his strange powers on the machines' decision-making centers.

"The *ES 110* must be regarded as a total loss," the robot told Buchanan. "Shall I repeat and beam to the cruisers?"

Wearily, Buchanan assented.

The somber message began to seep through the Singularity's weird fields, but even as it went, Maran's eyes narrowed to pinpoints and, like a clarion-call, his voice rang around the bridge of the station:

"This is Commander Maran! Your orders are to build a Quasi-warp capable of withstanding the discontinuous zones!"

Buchanan clutched at the straw. *Quasi-warp*?

"Repeat, please, Commander Maran," said the flat metallic voice of the Grade One robot.

"Build a Quasi-warp!"

"Elucidate, please, Commander."

Buchanan was ahead of the machines. The machines had said that they could not warp aside the chaotic, billowing fields of the Singularity. It was impossible. Inconceivable.

So Maran had ordered an approximation of a warp.

A Quasi-warp. One that might be possible.

It was a form of words. Don't try to make the impossible, Maran was ordering. Build on the data from the interior of the Singularity and make an approximation of that!

Maran's steadying, insidious, soothing, irresistible arguments followed, and, within seconds, the station jangled into hectic movement. Scanners ranged into the pit. Comps boiled with data. Engines began to flex for the first impulses; makeshift force-fields edged out into the strange void; a whole new dimensional framework began to invest the ship.

Then, like a sword-thrust, a great band of white-gold translucence cut through the boiling fields of the Singularity. It sliced aside the threatening serpentine coils and bathed the dying prison-ship in a sheath of strange radiance.

A scanner showed Buchanan the whole scene.

From the squat station an eerie, hauntingly beautiful tunnel had been pushed out toward the wreck of the *ES 110.* Around the three engines of the station hung a flowering, rippling surge of black light. Immense floods of power held the white-gold tunnel in place.

"He's done it," Buchanan whispered, between relief and incredulity. Then: "Liz!"

A freak of beaming showed her slim figure. Maran, directing a herd of low-grade servitors, hid her at first. He moved aside as the robots brought a small life-raft to the last part of the ship to resist the unreal dimensions. And then Buchanan saw Liz.

An impassive low-grade robot was hurrying her into deep-space armor. Buchanan yelled to her, but she did not see him. She looked dazed, altogether helpless.

Anger began then. Buchanan's craggy face was set in a cold mask. Mostly, the anger was directed at himself. Had he been harder—had he put the safety of his fellowmen first, he would not have allowed Maran to take control of his command.

A man of sterner spirit would have sacrified even a Liz Deffant.

Maran was loose.

Then Buchanan saw what a trap the station was.

Maran might be loose. He was not free.

"Commander Lientand to all cruisers," the Enforcement Service commander was saying. "I have a message from the Jansky Singularity Station to say that the *ES 110* is a total loss. Buchanan reports that there is a remote possibility of survivors. He's standing by."

As the *ES 110*'s screens imploded, Lientand completed his orders to the cruiser squadron:

"I repeat, keep to allotted patrol stations. All cruisers to carry out necessary steps with regard to the expellee Maran."

CHAPTER 16

"Commander Maran," said the Grade One robot from the Jansky Station, "my high-grade colleague aboard the *ES 110* is ready to assist in the completion of Quasi-warp. Kindly stand by for removal of sections of the bridge."

Liz Deffant almost giggled at the punctilious observance of niceties among machines which were disobeying their primary conditioning. She tried to operate the controls of the deep-space armor. It added an element of lunatic comedy when she began to float on a small force-screen toward the blank screen.

"Miss Deffant, please," said Maran, gigantic in the armored suit. "Into the raft, Miss Deffant."

A low-grade casually hooked her toward the small port as a gang of servitors ripped away the sides of the ship. Liz gasped with sudden pain as a blinding white-gold translucence flooded the wreckage. It was crazily beautiful, a zany dance of white and gold particles against sinking chains of hypercubes. "Quasi-warp," she said, half stunned.

Maran lumbered into the confined space of the raft, his movements energetic in spite of the weight of the armored suit. Liz glimpsed a tentacle flashing across the wrecked bridge to close the port of the makeshift raft. It was the last she saw of the *ES 110*, for the eerie flow of white-gold particles enveloped the entire ship. The strange translucence seeped into the raft too, finding invisible gaps and irradiating the cramped interior with its uncanny presence.

"This vessel is now defunct," said the robotic controller of the *ES 110*.

It was the only epitaph the prison-ship received.

Liz was flung hard against the side of the tiny craft as it lurched into the broken dimensions with a mind-reeling plunge. The raft spun wildly for a few seconds, and then it was grinding down the Quasi-warp tunnel away from the wreck of the *ES 110*. Liz looked at Maran and saw that his armored suit was crawling with the glittering, eerie radiance. He had the look of a monstrous god riding a chariot of suns.

Buchanan felt the absence of the station's protective screens with a deep-space voyager's instinctive alarm. The station quaked in the maelstrom. Engines howled with the effort of projecting the warp which could not exist. And which had been manufactured.

Scanners showed the breakup of the *ES 110*.

A fresh flurry of starquake grabbed the prison-ship and drew what was left of its shattered hulk inward. Buchanan caught the last unconcerned message from its robotic controller. There was a faint blast as the *ES 110* imploded.

Buchanan shivered. Any shipwreck was a desolating thing. There would be only broken fragments of this vessel to sink into the time-lost graveyard where the *Altair Star* lay. And then, through the showering debris and the fury of starquake, Buchanan glimpsed the hauntingly beautiful tunnel. It grew like some living thing in the broken dimensions, a tube of white-gold translucence that seemed too fragile to endure against the devastating onrush of serpentine coils billowing from the depths of the Singularity. Yet it held.

It held, and the engines of the station kept the wildness of starquake back. And the life-raft slowly crept toward the station. It lurched forward at first, but then its progress was slow, as if it fought painfully against an alien element; Buchanan breathed in shallow gulps as he thought of Liz Deffant encased in the frail pellet of a ship that was being reborn through the coruscating tube.

He was in the station's small hold when the raft nudged into the lock. A strange delirium of hope gripped him. When the battered raft creaked to a rest and the white-gold translucence died away, he could not contain himself.

"Liz! Liz!"

The two low-grade servitors that were the entire complement of the station went about their work efficiently. They assisted the two dazed figures from the raft and began to remove the massive space armor. Buchanan was taut with almost unendurable emotion. He heard the robotic controller of the station announce:

"Commander, starquake emissions dying down. Quasi-warp fields have been withdrawn. All three engines have resumed normal functions. There has been a slight failure of some elements of Number Two Engine, but maintenance systems have repairs in hand. Full efficiency will be obtained in all systems in one hour. What are your instructions?"

Buchanan was beside her as the helmet came free. Her long hair flowed around a pale face. She blinked and stared at him. A tension that had built up during the hours of the *ES 110*'s lunging voyage into the Singularity now burst, and Buchanan reached out a big, wide hand to touch her face.

He felt tears.

"Al—" whispered the girl, and he felt his senses battered. The touch of her soft skin was the revival of all he had ever hoped for. The *Altair Star* was only a distant, thin ghost, one that could stay in its shadowy nonlife. This was real, this tactile impression of her tears.

He saw her eyes fill with alarm and remembered that Maran was on his ship. He turned, fast.

"What are your instructions?" asked the robotic controller. "Sir, have you any instructions regarding *ES 110* personnel?"

Buchanan was himself again, alert and decisive. "I resume full command of the station," he snapped. "Full restraint procedures—seize the criminal expellee Maran and take him for medical attention. He is not to be permitted to speak—do not allow him to communicate with any automatic system!"

"Al, he controls—" Liz yelled, as Buchanan took a step toward the burly figure.

"What are your instructions, Commander?" the metallic flat voice interrupted, as Liz was shouting.

Buchanan opened his mouth to roar at the stupidity of the machines when he saw that the blank faces of the two low-grade servitors were not turned to him. In that moment, he knew what Liz was trying to say.

"Relinquish all decision-making procedures!" he called abruptly. "I am commander of this ship—accept no orders but mine!"

It was too late.

"Commander?" asked the robotic controller.

Both low-grades faced Maran. They were awaiting his orders. Like dogs, they knew their master.

Buchanan tried to reach Maran. His hands were wedge-shaped, the hard edges downward, the muscles in his shoulders and arms ready to power the blows that would crush Maran while he was still dazed from the mind-reeling passage of the tunnel.

It was always too late.

"Restrain," said Maran hoarsely.

Tentacles snaked to encompass Buchanan's limbs. He stared at him as two metallic carapaces regarded him indifferently. Buchanan felt anger surge within him once more, and again the anger was directed at himself. He had acted with such stupidity that it was hardly believable.

Maran had issued commands before leaving the *ES 110*. Of course he had! But he had been vulnerable for a few seconds when the life-raft lay like a stranded monster in the hold of the station; the man had been half crazed by the shock of the strange phenomenon of Quasi-warp. That should have been his chance, Buchanan thought savagely. He had lost it.

A sense of unreality gripped him. Here he was, in his own command, a prisoner of his own servitors. Facing him was the bulk of Maran, one of the most dangerous men ever to be sent to the Rim. By a freak of chance, Liz Deffant was here too—she had been brought across the spiraling arms of the Galaxy to this encounter, having played some part in the desperate events leading to Maran's presence.

Shocked, enraged, bewildered, he shouted to the robots: "I am Buchanan, commander of the station! Release me! I resume full control of all systems throughout the station! Maran is not to be allowed access to any system—secure him now!"

The tentacles did not relax. Buchanan's rage seeped away.

Both he and Liz were waiting for Maran to shake the sense-blinding effects of the Quasi-warp from his massive head. Haggard, patient, utterly fatigued, he at last looked directly at Buchanan. The sense of unreality would not leave Buchanan.

"Buchanan," Maran said, his strange deep eyes assessing the bound man before him. There was no hint of triumph. Buchanan could begin to appreciate the power of the man; another, in his place, would have shown pride, perhaps boasted of his mastery of the machines. Maran accepted the situation and his dominance of it; it was his right. About him, there was an aura of grandeur that was only partly to be explained by his size.

He was uninterested in fighting Buchanan. He would

not accept him as an opponent, in spite of the defiance in Buchanan's face. Any kind of confrontation was ruled out by his monumental patience.

Buchanan clung to his one advantage. "You can't get away," he said. "This station has no deep-space Phase capability. And Commander Lientand's squadron is waiting."

Maran was unperturbed. Like Liz, he was swaying. He was almost on the point of collapse. "Attend to Miss Deffant," he said. "You'll do that?"

"What?"

Liz Deffant heard. She was too tired to begin to explain.

"Yes," said Maran. "A remarkable woman." He gestured to the servitors, and the tentacles flowed away into invisible orifices. "The machines will hold you if you attempt to harm me," he said. "Be a realist, Buchanan. I must have rest—Miss Deffant will tell you about her trials aboard the prison-ship. When I have recovered, your machines will tell me about your command. In the meanwhile, do nothing rash."

Buchanan tensed, and an almost undetectable robotic quivering told him that the contraction of muscle had been noted. Maran was massively unimpressed.

"The robots will watch, Buchanan," he said. His deep eyes were wells of tiredness. "You were appointed to this station, presumably, Buchanan, because you have an expert knowledge of these tools." He indicated the low-grade servitors. "Respect them!"

"He's right," said Liz slowly. "He's always right."

Buchanan could not resist saying: "You won't get away, Maran." Childish as it was, the threat did something to restore his confidence.

"Very possibly," agreed Maran. "To the bridge," he ordered a servitor. It aided his halting progress to the small grav-chute. Buchanan was sure he was asleep before the chute took him to the bridge of the Jansky Station.

When he was gone, Buchanan looked down at his bony hands. He felt the crab of helplessness stirring in his body, gripping, clawing at him. Despair and doom echoed through his skull.

"Al?" whispered Liz, and he saw that she was exhausted.

Confused and bitter as he was, he responded to the appeal. Liz's eyes held no condemnation, only an urgent need. She lifted her arms and he bent to hold her. Minutes passed. Only the slow whine of remote systems could be heard. The ship might have held no more than the two of them. Buchanan felt a suffusion of delight such as he had never, not in the best days of their relationship, believed possible. It was a bursting of happiness that drowned the crablike clawings deep in his body.

Liz gently pushed Buchanan away. They had both drawn strength from the tenderness of reconciliation.

"I was a fool," whispered Buchanan, still amazed at the freak of coincidence that had kept her from joining the long-dead in the time-lost tunnel. "Why did I leave you?"

'You had to! I know how it was, Al!"

Buchanan saw that she had changed. There was a new edge of resolution about Liz Deffant. He remembered the cruiser commander's message.

"Maran?" he said. "He held you hostage?"

"No. I don't think so."

"When I think of him—"

"Don't—not now!"

"We have to!"

"There's been too much, Al! Too much for anyone to take!"

He held her, lightly this time. But even during this second long embrace, Maran's brooding presence made itself felt. A robotic voice said peremptorily:

"Routine report, Commander Buchanan!"

"Well?"

He hardly had time to ask himself if the machines had revertedly to his authority before it demolished the unborn hope.

"Commander Maran wishes you to listen to all routine reports, sir. The latest on core emission is that condition starquake is now in abeyance. There are simple dipole configurations and data corresponding with previous readings. No aberrant energy fields. That is all, sir."

Buchanan heard, filled with a sharp self-disgust. Maran had instructed the machines to keep him informed. He was, possibly, useful to the cyberneticist who had so easily taken his ship from him. Maran slept, confident of the robots' loyalty.

He heard a racking sob and saw that Liz Deffant was at the end of her powers of endurance. Cursing himself for his selfishness, he led her to the grav-chute. A tentacle restrained him gently.

"Let me pass," he ordered.

"Commander Buchanan will remain in the hold until summoned by Commander Maran," it informed him.

Buchanan shrugged. "Get a couch for Miss Deffant."

"Yes, sir."

Liz was talking now. Some of the story came out, garbled and incoherent: ". . . he was so young! And those hands . . . but he had to do it! It was the animal that took over. . . . Al, he wasn't responsible—but the eyes! The eyes in the cell-deck—all staring! It was green, Al—they were thrashing about and dying! But he had to do it that way! It's the small-minded bigots who had him sent out! If he's given a chance, he can change the nature of our minds! And poor Tup's neck—it broke, *broke*!"

Al stopped the flow of words as her voice rose to an hysterical pitch. He could only guess at the horrors of the doomed ship's last hours. Murder. The successive shocks of the cruisers' combined fields. The escape of the wounded prison-ship commander. She should not go through the trauma of telling it, not yet.

He soothed her, comforting her by his physical presence.

"Rosario?" she asked abruptly.

"He was picked up. I had a message from the commander of the cruiser. He's safe and well."

And then she was back in the nightmare. "I tried, Al—I found a gun—a musket, and I've never killed anything in my life—but I tried to kill him!"

"All right! Now rest! Tell me later!"

"But I tried to kill him!" She was trying to make him understand with an agony of desperation.

"Liz, I would have done the same!"

"But *him*!"

And Buchanan knew she was in a frenzied torment.

"Forget him! Rest now—sleep!"

"The musket fired—he knew!"

Buchanan began to worry. This was more than fatigue, more than understandable nervous reaction to even mayhem. Liz was in a state of acute anxiety over Maran.

"Not now, Liz," he said. "Leave it!"

"I tried—to—kill—Maran."

Buchanan thought of what he knew of Maran. A powerful and hypnotic personality, a man with a unique charisma, a man who could exert such a power over the minds of men and women that they volunteered willingly for the brutal surgery his machines inflicted on the deepest centers of the cortex. They died believing they were Maran's disciples.

Liz?

She was staring at him with a shocked despair.

She had tried to kill Maran. And, because of that attempt, she was suffering from an unholy feeling of guilt that would not give her the slightest remission.

Buchanan sensed the right thing to say. Hating himself, but able to say the words to the woman he loved, he whispered: "He forgave you. Liz, Maran forgave you."

Liz's anguish diminished. Gradually the panic left her eyes. "Yes," she whispered back. "He did." She slept.

Buchanan kicked out savagely at the watchful servitor. Even as his legs braced to take the impact of its metallic bulk, a tentacle swept out to hold him. Another prevented him from falling.

He sat down to watch Liz sleep. He had found her again, only to lose her to the mesmeric genius who had taken his ship.

The three of them were trapped, he and Liz doubly trapped. And where was the way out for any of them?

CHAPTER 17

Watching Liz Deffant slowly emerge from a deep sleep, Buchanan had the curious impression that none of the events leading up to Maran's presence aboard the station had happened. Time telescoped. They were together, and they seemed not to have separated. Liz looked tired, of course; they were in the cramped hold of the station; a servitor followed their every slightest movement; but they were the same people, he and Liz. They had a planned future.

Buchanan frowned. Except that Liz seemed to be under Maran's spell. It was a matter he would have to approach with care. Maran himself was a different thing entirely; if only there was some weapon he could use against him! But it was out of the question. The responses of the automatons were measured in ten-thousandths of a second; Maran was right to rely on their lightning reactions.

Then Liz opened her eyes and Buchanan could relax for a moment.

The panic and despair were gone.

Buchanan had always appreciated her levelheaded, gentle, persistent way of thinking. He respected her intellect. He had known her achieve better results than cleverer colleagues because she did not try too hard. She allowed her mind to range over a problem, letting an answer emerge by a slow process of growth. Buchanan could see that she had recovered her balance. However, he would not broach the question of her feelings about Maran.

"Liz, I'd like to know more about what happened—I know some of it," he said. "I'd like to know so that I can think of some way of getting us out of this mess."

"Al, we can't do anything."

He hadn't expected this calmness. "No?"

"No, Al. We have to leave decisions to Maran now."

Complete resignation, thought Buchanan. It was bad. "I tried to establish control while you slept."

"It's no use, Al. I've thought a lot about it." A memory swam through her mind. An almost perfect humanoid, hair receding, smiling, concerned, knowing all about her. The clerk at Bookings had known exactly what she wanted, who she was, where she had been. "It was all too easy," she went on, and Buchanan again felt hollow at the degree of resignation in her voice. "He knew that the robots would obey him."

"Maran?"

She went on: "He must have had only a minute or two in which to gain control of the cell-deck. It couldn't have been longer. There would have been automatic alarms, and the cruisers would have easily caught up with the ship."

"It shouldn't have happened at all," agreed Buchanan. "The prison-ships are triple-protected by fail-safes. He couldn't have got to them." He attempted lightness: "When we get out of this, we'll live primitive. No machines. You do the cooking, I'll cut the wood. If a machine comes near, I'll get it to abort itself."

Liz smiled, and Buchanan almost groaned with relief.

"Maran must have prepared, Al. Don't you see, it was all too easy for him! He must have had contingency plans. I don't believe he could have taken over the machines in so short a space of time—he must have foreseen that he would be taken out to the Rim on an automatic ship. Al, the machines know *everything*! They're all mutually compatible."

Buchanan saw now. Maran would have got to the Enforcement Service central memory-banks. There would have been some kind of delay-circuit.

"Yes. That's how he did it."

"And the hypno-sleep conditioning—with a mind like his he could evolve a mental and physical simulation of conditioning. Drugs—an alteration of his neural patterns—and an instruction to the high-grade robots to cut in when the *ES 110* was deep into the gulfs.

"And I let him take over my ship."

Liz was still wondering at Maran's genius. "I've worked with the Grade One machines. They're sophisticated. I sometimes think they have their own emergent personalities. They frighten me. But Maran could get to them. He must have contingency plans for when he gets away from the Singularity."

"He can't!" Buchanan could not allow it to pass.

"You don't know him," she answered quietly. "He's more than human."

"There's no way out for him. Not with cruisers patrolling the entire Quadrant. There'll be a network of ships and beacons out there until the station can't support itself within the Singularity. It can't get free—there just isn't the Phase capability. We're trapped; he's trapped, Liz." He hesitated. "You wouldn't want him free?"

Liz was troubled. The air of fanaticism she had worn when he first saw her had gone; but she was deeply disturbed by the strange encounter with Maran.

"Free again, Liz—Maran?" he prompted.

"I didn't want you to waste your life looking for a ghost-ship."

"That," said Buchanan, realizing how little it meant to him now.

"I couldn't stop you. We can't stop Maran. We shouldn't."

"No, Liz?"

"I don't know!" she burst out. "He's done terrible things—I saw him squeeze the life out of a young crewman! But he shouldn't be put away like an animal—not a mind like his! Al, he has qualities that we can't begin to understand!"

"He did things to men and women that shouldn't be done."

"I know!"

Buchanan did not press her. The wildness was in her eyes again. They glowed golden, helpless, full of doubts and confusion.

"He is different," admitted Buchanan. "It was impossible that this ship could project any kind of warp in the conditions that existed a few hours ago. But he told the machines to make a hypothetical warp, a Quasi-warp as he called it, and they did it. Yet there's still no way out for him."

"I thought he wanted me as a hostage," said Liz.

"Lientand wouldn't consider bargaining with—"

"No! Maran wouldn't bargain either." She said, puzzled: "He wanted me to stay on the *ES 110*—he could have had me released when he sent the survival-cylinders out, but he didn't. I think he wanted someone with him.

Maybe as a witness, Al. Someone he could explain his conduct to—someone who would be able to report that he acted as he did because he was, simply, Maran."

Buchanan thought of the man's deep eyes, his imposing bulk, the way he had shaken his massive head to free it of the jangling residues of the sense-blinding fields he had passed through. What did he intend now?

"If I hadn't been so blind!" he groaned. "To think I started this!"

Impulsively, Liz Deffant reached across to him: "I told you I understand now, Al. You had to go—truly, Al, I know it."

It was the thought of the Quasi-warp that made Buchanan tell Liz about the *Altair Star*. There was a link that he could not yet comprehend, one that he was not aware of having thought of as possible; nevertheless, the memory of that beacon-bright eerie field growing out toward the failing transport had something to do with the time-lost liner.

"I saw it," he said. "I saw the ship."

Liz felt a surge of resentment. It passed. The lost ship was no barrier between them anymore.

"The remains of the *Altair Star*?" she asked.

"The ship itself," he insisted. "It didn't break up, like the *ES 110*."

"It's intact?"

"It's with a fleet of other ships—ships lost for a thousand years, Liz."

Liz knew the dreadful turmoil of spirit that Buchanan had endured three years before. Was he suffering from some sort of hallucination brought on by grief and loneliness? She looked and saw the active intelligence in his eyes, not the visionary excitement of a Maran.

"Did you reach the ship, Al?"

"No. I caught a glimpse of a kind of ships' graveyard—dozens of ancient ships. They were held in some kind of time-tunnel, some weird effect of the Singularity. I saw it, but the robots wouldn't have it that it could exist. They said it was impossible. There couldn't be such a temporal discontinuity."

Liz grappled with the idea. Cosmic events surrounded her. A bizarre genius had taken over a prison-ship and hurtled with it into the Singularity; at the Singularity, Al could talk, more or less calmly, about a strange tunnel of time. And Al, trained field man, talented beyond so many in his area of research, had not been able to persuade the robots that what he had seen could exist.

"It was like a hole in the fabric of the Universe," went on Buchanan. "It was so utterly alien that I could not begin to explain what it was."

"It still troubles you?"

Buchanan felt his own unsureness. He had been ready to forget the *Altair Star* and its ghosts. If it had been possible for them to leave the Singularity, he could have left the mystery unsolved. There was no prospect of that, though.

Liz watched him. Buchanan's ghosts were not laid, whatever he said. The finding of the *Altair Star* was only the beginning of Al's new tribulations.

"You would go to the ship—if you could?"

"It's impossible." But he had said that before. There was something that he should remember. . . .

"But you'd go?"

"I keep seeing the faces!" he burst out.

"Did you see anything in the ship?"

"Not the passengers or crew. But it was exactly as I remember it. There was no further deterioriation of its fabric. It's exactly as it was when I saw it go into the Singularity—into that weird field!"

"Al, I've told you I truly understand. I couldn't before. Now I know how these ideas can hold one."

Buchanan was back in time. "If I'd been able to get down to the engines—if I'd thought of wrecking the memory-banks sooner—maybe I could have worked something out!"

Liz was near to weeping with pity for him. "Does it matter so much, Al? It's all long gone!"

Buchanan looked at her. There was more, she thought. Deep lines she had not seen for years were etched into his face.

"They may not have gone."

"They?"

"Nearly seven hundred men, women, and children."

"Al, they must have been dead for three years! You can't help them!" Liz felt a sense of cold inevitability. A shadowy horror hung over Al Buchanan, and it was creeping out to envelop her too.

"I wasn't going to tell you."

"Tell me."

"Kochan made the station possible."

"Why?"

"His granddaughter was a passenger."

"Tell me, Al."

"His scientists came up with a theory about the Singularity."

"This—tunnel?"

Buchanan told her. "Time might hold still."

"And if it does, then she—"

"—and all the others. Still there."

There was a horror, thought Liz. Death was the constant companion of them all. It was the thought of not dying that was peculiarly horrible.

"A theory, Al—only a theory, you say!" She was shuddering.

"I have to make sure."

"Maran—he won't be interested in the tunnel! You won't be able to go to the *Altair Star*, Al!"

Buchanan's craggy face was ugly with bitterness. While his mind had been ranging over the amazing glimpse of the *Altair Star*, he had experienced one of those moments which come, with rare and fortunate intuition, to trained field men when they are faced with irreconcilable sets of data and conflicting theories. A double mystery might, just might, be explicable. Maran's abrupt orders; the frenzied activity of the machines; the building of the eerie Quasiwarp; the time-lost tunnel which the robots would not record. Memories, ideas, projections had surged and coalesced and strayed together. Buchanan was sure of what he said.

"Maran will want to see the *Altair Star*."

"What!"

"Yes, Liz."

Staring at the man she still loved, Liz thought she would never be able to follow his thoughts. She sagged back on the couch. She might have lain until she slept had not a robotic voice called deferentially to them. A weird, overpolite invitation brought her to her feet.

"Commander Buchanan and Miss Deffant. Commander Maran presents his compliments. He would be honored if they would dine with him immediately. This system requires confirmation," it added.

Buchanan put an arm around Liz Deffant's shoulders. "This, Liz," he said, "will be something to tell them about when we're back at Center."

He could not understand why Liz began to sob uncontrollably until she said: "Tup said the same thing!" Jerkily, she went on: "It was the first time I saw Maran! He said it would be something to tell them about when I got home! And he's dead!"

"We're coming," Buchanan said grimly to the servitor. There was no way to comfort Liz. She would have to learn to live with her own ghosts.

CHAPTER 18

The meal was a parody of a dinner party. The servitors passed around the food and wine with the deferential air of family retainers. Maran headed a table like some patriarch. He ate and drank with gusto, politely attentive at all times to Liz, and complimentary to Buchanan on the excellence of his judgment in selecting appetizing meal-programs. He would not allow a discussion of their future until the robots deftly flicked away the last of the dishes.

"Coffee, Miss Deffant?" he inquired. "And try some of Mr. Buchanan's brandy. Excellent!" he added, sipping the fine liqueur. "You'll appreciate that I have not been able to enjoy the pleasures of the table in recent months. The Enforcement Service have a puritanical approach to refreshment. Their attitude is a hangover from less enlightened times than our own."

Buchanan cautioned himself against an outburst. Maran's treatment of them had been utterly correct. There had been no threats, no demands. And though he had taken over the station, he had treated Liz and himself as honored guests. What could one do in the face of such unpatronizing confidence?

"No doubt you will be thinking of the time when the Service again has me in its charge?" Maran inquired, uncannily picking up Buchanan's unspoken retort.

"I can't see how you can evade the cruisers," Buchanan answered. "The station has a limited capacity for life-support. The cruisers can keep on patrol in relays. As soon as the station tries to leave the peripheries of the Singularity, it can be picked up by force-screens. Your escape is temporary, Maran."

Liz Deffant looked from one man to the other. Both were impressive, both resolute and determined. She had no doubt which would triumph in any contest. Maran's single-mindedness would be supreme. She could only be a spectator now.

Maran exerted his personality when he spoke again to Buchanan. "I have told Miss Deffant that I have the feeling that you, she, and I were predetermined to meet, Buchanan."

"So we've met," said Buchanan tightly.

Maran smiled. "Buchanan, I know the conditioning you Galactic Service personnel receive. But try to break out of it for a few moments—forget what you have heard of Maran the monster. Think of what you see before you—look!"

And Maran was a smiling, easy host, glass in hand and relaxed smile creasing his big, broad face. Liz Deffant saw the deep, hypnotic eyes and wondered at the strange influence he had over her. Since he had first explained his tormented vision, she had been unable to summon up a jot of resolution or courage. Looking at Maran was like being faced with some stupendous force of nature.

"I heard what you did," said Buchanan. "You can't be allowed to rip the minds from any more men and women. Even though they are willing."

Maran nodded slowly. "My machines are crude. They are not yet ready for the delicate work of examining the cells which carry an imprint of man's evolutionary processes. They harm, they maim, and, regrettably, they destroy. I won't pretend that Maran has not brought misery and death to the noble spirits who followed him. But, Buchanan, there has to be a start! We must examine the deep centers that alone carry the impression of that moment of transition that made us what we are! One day, Buchanan, cell-surgery will be a commonplace—but only if a start is made! And Maran has made the start! And Maran will find a way through the mists of time and isolate that moment of change. Miss Deffant," he said, turning to Liz. "You believe that Maran can do it?"

Buchanan saw the answering gleam in Liz's eyes.

She said nothing, but he knew that she was Maran's.

"It isn't my decision," Buchanan said. "But if it were, I'd stop you. And send you out to the Rim." He paused. "If I had to, Maran, I'd destroy you."

As he said it, he knew that, if he felt a bitter antagonism toward Maran, it was not for his treatment of those who had volunteered to take part in his strange experiments. It was more simple, more basic, than that. Maran had woven a spell on the woman Buchanan wanted more than anything in the Universe. Jealousy, he recognized. He was jealous of Maran!

"Would you?" asked Liz quietly. "Would you, Al?"

He turned away from the hurt in the golden eyes.

"Al—you couldn't. I know," she said. "You just haven't got the hate in you, Al."

"A fruitless conversation," sighed Maran. "I had hoped for better things."

Buchanan felt choked by his conflicting emotions. There was a need for violent action very near the surface of his mind; yet the robots hovered close, ready to react with instant speed. *Patience*, he warned himself. Maran had not yet spoken of what he intended to do. The station had a considerable capacity for life-support, but that capacity had to be divided by three now that Maran and Liz were aboard. Maran could do simple equations too.

Liz asked the question that dominated Buchanan's thoughts: "Well, what do you intend to do, Maran? Al's right—the cruisers can't let you escape. Commander Lientand can sit outside the Singularity until you're ready to give up. There's no way out."

"I think Buchanan knows," said Maran.

Buchanan said nothing, did not allow a movement of his face to betray his thoughts.

"Al?" asked Liz.

"I checked the reports, Buchanan," said Maran. "All the readings."

"I expected that," agreed Buchanan.

Yet what could Maran do, even if he persuaded the machines that what was clearly impossible might be reached?

"Al?" asked Liz again.

"Buchanan feels it his duty not to discuss the object of his search," said Maran.

"You said you wouldn't—"

"Don't!" Buchanan said harshly.

"Buchanan, I know!" Maran said decisively. "Yes, Miss Deffant. I told you I felt a sense of predestination about your involvement with my escape from the *ES 110*. Our paths coincide."

"The ship?" she said, trembling.

"Yes, Miss Deffant. I shall invite Commander Buchanan to return with me to his former command. I have instructed the machines to take us to the *Altair Star*."

Liz gasped. Buchanan's fist clenched around the stem of the glass. The slender stem snapped in his hand, and brandy made a spreading stain. A servitor had the cloth cleared and the brandy mopped away within seconds.

"When?" asked Buchanan.

"Why, when you have finished your drink," said Maran, as the robot placed another glass before Buchanan.

Liz Deffant saw the massive, serpentine coils enveloping the station and gripped Buchanan's arm until the nails bit into the flesh; an unreasoning panic blotted out all other thoughts. Buchanan swayed too, knowing that no matter how many times he ventured within the deeper reaches of the bizarre space-time enigma he could never become accustomed to the appalling blank *otherness* at the center. He saw that Maran was stunned by the violence of the descent into the Singularity.

And there was nothing he could do, for the slender tentacles of the couch held him firm.

The station shuddered, engines howling, as the drive built force-screens to ease the station through a vicious conjunction of energies. The big screen showed the coils giving way to a whirling blackness shot through with emerald whorls. From the black pit, reinforcing bands of power emerged to investigate the nugget of human technology which had invaded the Singularity.

The station exuded screens, leaking power and easing between colossal forces. And it slid away, away and nearer the center.

Through eerie vortices, countering brute power with subtle field emissions, the station glided smoothly into the bizarre regions. Buchanan breathed a prayer of relief and gratitude to the engineers who had built the ship. They had been able only to guess at the grim fury of the Singularity's inner depths, but they had planned and built well. No engine failed, no screen slipped.

The ship became calmer, its pace less subject to wild upheavals. Maran could concentrate on the operations screen, while Buchanan watched him.

There was no sign that he was afraid. If he trembled, it was not from fear, but awe at the incredible violence of the Singularity, and the miracle of the little ship's survival.

The maelstrom surged, and Maran's face showed both

awe and excitement. Buchanan stared now at the screen. He saw the strange black depths and felt his mind reeling.

"Look!" roared Maran, and Liz and Buchanan were held in a trance by the stark emptiness of the blackness at the center of the Singularity. They glimpsed it and shut their eyes.

"An entire new Universe!" Maran shouted.

But his two companions could not look. Reluctantly, Buchanan conceded Maran a measure of greatness. The bizarre architecture of the Singularity was a fit context for him. Maran was unquestionably awed by what he had seen, but he had lost none of his assurance. Massively excited, he radiated confidence and power.

"Al!" whispered Liz as Maran lowered his great head to the command console. "Al, why does he want to go to the *Altair Star*?"

Buchanan saw that Maran was indifferent to them. Eyes half closed, he was staring raptly at the screen.

"The ship's almost intact," he said. "If he could reach it, he could use the engines to power a life-raft."

"But you can't let him—Al, it's like a mausoleum, you said! No one should disturb them!"

Buchanan felt the sick excitement of his quest welling up inside him once more. Cursing his inconstancy, he whispered: "I don't want to go, Liz—I don't want Maran to have a chance of freedom! But I have to go!"

It seemed to take hours, but only minutes passed. Buchanan watched the seconds fly away and wondered if time were structured differently in the inner depths. Speculation was futile. No satisfactory theory had explained the unreal dimensions. Kochan's words came back to him, and there was an uncanny stirring of the skin and short hair behind his ears. He shuddered, as Liz had done, recalling the idea of the long undead. It was a betrayal of the natural order of things.

And yet there was still the gripping compulsion to return to the *Altair Star*. It could not be denied. Whatever he might find, and however much he dreaded it, he had to go on now that he was so near. Even though Maran meant to use the ship!

Green-glowing serpentine coils gave way to infinite emptiness.

They were near the mystery now, very close to the strange stars, or the black hole, or the combination of unguessable events that formed the center of the enigma.

Buchanan saw the *Altair Star* as the eerie tunnel swam onto the big screen. A flickering glimpse, and then it was gone. Liz saw it.

"Al!" breathed Liz Deffant, cutting into his thoughts and bringing a rush of feelings that he could not concern himself with now.

"This is the place of wrecks?" asked Maran.

"This is the place."

Scanners roamed as Maran manipulated the sensor-pads.

"Readings," he demanded.

"No starquake emission," reported the Grade One robot. "All three engines operating at satisfactory levels of efficiency. Screens engaged at nine-point-three-one-eight-two level."

"Report the condition of the *Altair Star*."

"Sir?"

"They don't admit the scan," said Buchanan.

"Report on the tunnel," said Maran, ignoring Buchanan's objection.

"The tunnel, sir?" asked the Grade One robot.

"They won't admit the temporal discontinuity," Buchanan said. "Nothing. No tunnel, no temporal discontinuity, so no ship."

Maran wove a spell over the console. Robotic systems hesitated. Buchanan did not doubt Maran's powers. As the big, white hands gentled the sensor-pads into compliance, the station edged nearer the glittering tunnel. The screens were filled with an astonishing glory. Then, Buchanan again glimpsed the emptiness that lay a whole Universe beyond the strange glittering tunnel. He saw a terrifying emptiness that sent his thoughts awry and brought a spangled, reeling and roaring confusion inside his mind.

When it cleared, Maran was giving orders in his calm, insistent voice: "Scan."

"Sir?" asked the robotic controller.

"For ships."

"I have intermittent contact-potential with three Enforcement Service cruisers, sir."

"Not those."

"I have readings of the debris of a large transport, with implosion immediately preceding breakup."

"The *ES 110*," said Buchanan.

Maran held up a hand to indicate that he should be silent. Two flat carapaces regarded Buchanan with no menace at all. Yet they conveyed alert tension. He gritted his teeth in frustration. *Patience*, he tried to tell himself. All led to the *Altair Star*. Once he had determined the fate of the hundreds he had led to their doom, he could begin to plan, estimate, take decisions, find the single chink in Maran's armor of self-confidence.

"Scan," repeated Maran.

"Sir?" asked the robot.

"The temporal discontinuity observed by Commander Buchanan."

"An interesting theory," said the flat, metallic voice. "One that Mr. Kochan supports. It is, of course, impossible, sir."

Maran did not hesitate: "Reduce screen levels."

"Yes, sir."

The station had an oddly defenseless feeling. Buchanan tensed again, aware of the gigantic forces that might boil up and leave the ship in submicroscopic, jangling fragments.

But it held.

"Project a warp to the temporal discontinuity," ordered Maran.

"To what, sir?"

"The discontinuity."

Buchanan sensed the rebelliousness of the Grade One robot. If it would not accept Maran's orders, they all faced Lientand's ships.

"With what object, sir?" the machine at last asked.

"Investigating a theory."

"Sir?"

Buchanan could almost hear the self-questioning of the robots.

Maran snapped: "Isn't that the object of the Jansky Singularity Station?"

"The object of the station is observation and recording, sir," the flat voice answered at once, quite certain now. "Those are the primary functions, sir."

"Then observe the temporal discontinuity!"

"Which cannot exist, sir!"

Liz Deffant saw the big man's utter concentration. His large, deep eyes were pinpoints as he stared at the pedestal which housed the Grade One robot.

"Observe the Quasi-discontinuity!"

"Sir?"

There was a long pause. Buchanan had seen the myriads of circuits, the endless tiny sheaves of memory-cells, which were the core of the ship's computers. There was more factual knowledge in them than a man could store in a million lifetimes. And it was all ready for instant recall. There were generative systems which could produce strategies to cope with any eventuality the machines could understand.

They had said they could not scan the impossible.

The discontinuity—the time-tunnel—was impossible.

Therefore, they reasoned, they could not cope with it. They could not admit its existence.

And Maran was telling them to scan for a time-tunnel which might exist—a hypothetical discontinuity.

Buchanan knew he would return to the *Altair Star* in that moment. It was a confirmation of Maran's prescience. Maran had ordered the impossible. And the machines accepted the order.

"Very good, sir," came the metal-edged voice.

They watched as the marvelous, haunting time-tunnel began to take shape. Bathed in a coruscating white-gold sea of strange, eddying forces, the ships appeared on the screen. Liz Deffant sighed.

She forgot the burly figure at the console. All the experiences of the bitter hours drifted from her memory. She saw what Al Buchanan had seen, and she entered into his knowledge, shared his wonder and grief, understood his compulsive obsession as never before. The eerie resting-place of so many ships was dreamily peaceful, utterly beyond anything she had thought to see. Al was right. It was alien but beckoning, terrifying but compelling. The mystery lay before her in its bizarre majesty.

A freak scanning showed the whole length of the *Altair Star*. Washed by ripples of white-gold translucence, it gleamed like some magnificent, somber tomb.

"We shouldn't disturb it," breathed Liz. "No, Al!"

"Please, Liz," said Buchanan.

Maran brought the scanners close to the ship. He knew ships. "The bridge has gone. But that doesn't mean she's a wreck."

"It was blasted clear. Against my orders."

"Yes," said Maran. "It was under robotic direction?"

"Infragalactic policy. I tried to take over."

Buchanan thought of the frenzied, despairing, harsh

orders, the gouging shocks as his engineers ripped out decision-making systems.

"And?"

"I took too long to make the decision to take over."

Maran frowned. "Power potential when you blasted clear?"

"About eight percent."

"Low."

"The robots let the screens down."

"Yes," said Maran.

"Leave the ship alone, Al! Please!" Liz said, turning to Maran.

"I'm sorry, Miss Deffant," Maran said.

Buchanan waited, bile in his mouth. The years of searing anguish, interrupted by Liz Deffant's tenderness, had led to this moment.

"Well?" he asked.

"We go, Buchanan."

"All of us?"

"Not Miss Deffant."

"Stay here," said Buchanan to Liz.

"We both have our reasons for going," Maran said to her. "Buchanan's you know. You may or may not have guessed mine. But you know this, Miss Deffant," and his great eyes were luminously intent. "You know that Maran must not fail!"

Liz shrank back, afraid for Al Buchanan, convulsively afraid that Maran might work some shocking legerdemain aboard the ghost-ship.

"Project a Quasi-warp," ordered Maran.

The robotic controller still hedged. "Where to, sir?"

"To the *Altair Star*!"

"We'll take deep-space armor," Buchanan added.

"Why?" asked Maran.

"Life-support. Aboard the *Altair Star*. Its systems should have run out." He said in a low voice: "I hope they have."

"I must state, for the purposes of record that the station commander is grossly exceeding the instructions of the Board," the Grade One robot announced.

Buchanan followed Maran to the hold.

Liz Deffant watched the ghostly fleet, picking out here a bulbous ion-fission hulk that had not roared across the dimensions for half a millenium; there an elegant scout that had drifted into the tunnel not more than sixty or seventy years before. She could hardly bare to look at the huge, infragalactic liner that had been Al Buchanan's command.

CHAPTER 19

The eerie journey brought a proximity desired by neither man, yet each derived a measure of comfort from the knowledge that another human being was in the cramped cabin. Pinpoints of white-gold iridescence spangled the interior. Its tiny engines groaned as shields were forced inward by the blossoming Quasi-warp. Coiling shards of black light began to build up as the glittering tunnel formed around the raft. The Singularity's fields jerked and pushed, and the raft spun crazily as it left the station.

Buchanan gave no thought to Maran. Half-forgotten scenes tumbled with appalling clarity through his mind: a child's toy; the stunned face of a dignified old man; Preston's refusal to believe that the machines would condemn them, his shout of protest. . . . The last moments of the *Altair Star* haunted him afresh. He could see the lost faces, the dawning horror, the slow realization that the final moment had come.

"Proceed," ordered Maran.

The Quasi-warp, created by the station's pulsing engines, reached out to the misty edges of the strange graveyard of ships.

Buchanan saw Maran's big-boned, overfleshed face through the visor. There was a grotesque magnificence in his bulk. His eyes burned with a deep, profound, and tormented vision. Buchanan knew that he should be considering his own future actions; he should be working on some way of thwarting Maran's escape plans. But he could not. Liz was safe. Whatever happened to Maran and himself aboard the *Altair Star*—and he was more sure than ever that he would reach the ship—she would be cared for.

The robots would safeguard her person. If he and Maran failed to return, they would decide that the station and its records should be preserved; and Liz with it. Perhaps Maran knew that only if Liz's safety was assured would he willingly accompany him to the riven, time-lost shop.

Buchanan firmly put down any speculation about what Maran wanted him for; it was enough that he was returning to his command. He would find the answer to the question that had tortured him for so many years, that had sustained him through the long interview with the Board, that had kept him intent and purposeful during the descents into the depths of the Singularity. Time enough to wonder about Maran when he had put to rest the ghosts of the *Altair Star*.

"Maran," he said urgently. "I want to be the first to step into my ship." He was pleading, but he did not care. "It was my command."

"Agreed," said Maran.

The Quasi-warp built into a thrusting, glowing spear that sliced through the unguessable forces. It merged with the strange architecture of the Singularity and allowed the life-raft to pass into the deeper regions. A small screen pulsed irregularly. Buchanan's mind spun as the screen picked out the fantastic time-locked graveyard.

"There!" he called.

They had reached the impossible temporal discontinuity. And the images of the ancient ships filled the screen—blurred, almost unrecognizable as the deep-space vessels to the untrained eye, but immediately identifiable to Buchanan. And Maran, it seemed.

"I see, Buchanan."

Maran fed in commands. The raft hung, shot through with the white-gold, stunning radiance and the eerie black light. Every cell in Buchanan's body seemed invested with the Singularity's weird effects. Yet he saw the ship.

"The *Altair Star*!"

The impossible warp drilled through and into the time-tunnel. Coruscating, whirling forces eddied around the raft as it glided along its sheath of translucence toward the *Altair Star*. Buchanan clung to the obsessive fixation that had worried and ripped at his mind for so long: why had the robots allowed so many to sink away into the glittering tunnel?

Then even that thought was gone as a sudden eddy of grotesque forces bent the Quasi-warp. Maran struggled to hold the raft, but the Singularity's weird forces would not be denied. The little craft was hurled about with a blind, brutal frenzy of strange powers. And the two men pitched about the tiny cabin helplessly.

Buchanan's mind reeled. He struggled for sanity, for breath, for memory. Then, there was peace.

Calmness came like an explosion.

There was the boiling tumult as the Quasi-warp merged with the bizarre equilibrium of forces that made up the time-locked tunnel; and then nothing. Utter calm possessed the life-raft.

"Take over," said Maran.

Buchanan forced his mind to clear and his hands to obey his will. But he trembled, the big gauntlets hardly able to manipulate the simple controls of the console. All was impatience, dread, incoherency, unplanned haste. Yet he could steer the battered raft through the gaping hole where the bridge of the *Altair Star* had once been. Terribly afraid, but unable to avoid facing the remains of the ship, he slid the raft with easy skill toward his last infragalactic command.

It was as bad as he had feared.

Buchanan ignored Maran's restraining hand. He clambered out of the raft and crossed the ruin of the deck. All about him, the tenuous energies of the Quasi-warp shimmered and coruscated in a weird merging with the white-gold of the eerie tunnel. There was an area of complete calm where the two sets of forces met. Buchanan walked toward the splayed figures of his crewmen.

Preston was there, frozen in the act of ripping out a bank of memory-coils. A crewman whose name he had never been able to remember was beside him. Both, he sensed, might move at the approach of his armored figure. Their limbs still seemed to have the elasticity of flesh and muscle that indicates life; Preston's hair tumbled over his face—Buchanan expected him to brush it from his eyes in the familiar half-irritated gesture he knew so well. Behind these two were other figures—crewmen, three other men Buchanan had seen in the passengers' lounges. Maybe they had some knowledge of the machines whose destruction Buchanan had ordered. Some held ripping tools. To the last, they had tried to save the ship.

Buchanan stopped, halted by an appalling, gruesome thought.

Were Kochan's theorists right?—were these splayed figures held in some kind of shadowy hinterland, between life and death? Was the blonde-haired girl with the haunted eyes somewhere beyond the wrecked bridge, waiting in a timeless moment for the death that should have come three years before? Was it the same all over the ship?

"No!" whispered Buchanan, afraid to go on. The huge liner might be a gigantic mausoleum, as Kochan believed. But one that held the undead. He yelled out in tormented grief, quintessential terror and primeval dread striking through him as he thought of the hundreds of unliving yet undying in their time-struck ranks throughout the riven ship. Events in time seemed to telescope once more, and he saw again the uncomprehending fears of the passengers turn to grim knowledge as the ship began its last, fluttering plunge into the Singularity.

He could say nothing, nor could he move.

His soul revolted.

How long he might have stood, huge in the deep-space armor, he could not tell; perhaps he might have gone beyond the pool of calmness formed by the Quasi-warp and toward the glittering, beckoning areas where the splayed bodies hung. It could have happened, for he was oppressed by a nightmarish surge of guilt, grief, and horror; a few steps would have taken him into the limbo where time seemed to have stopped.

Maran prevented any such move.

"Buchanan, I need you to direct the machines!" boomed the amplified voice.

Buchanan surfaced, leaving the waking dream.

Maran. Here, in the vast charnel-house. Maran intruding in this haunting and terrible place. It was unthinkable.

He must be got out.

Buchanan turned and broke into a lunging run.

"Stop!" boomed the vast voice. "Think of Miss Deffant, Buchanan—think of yourself! Think of this ship!"

And Buchanan, having no thoughts at all, only a sense of outrage, was halted by the sheer confidence of Maran's orders. He was brought back to a measure of sanity, and he could recall his situation, that of Liz Deffant, why and how he had reached the *Altair Star* and what he was to do about the pitiful, silent remains of the liner's crew and passengers.

"Buchanan, this Quasi-warp protects us, you and me! But it can't hold for long! I need you to help me get the robots to build a drive, Buchanan! I haven't got enough time to redirect their programs. Help me, Buchanan, and you return to Miss Deffant at the station!"

Buchanan stared at the armored figure. He could see Maran's anxiety. Turn Maran loose? Certainly the *Altair Star*'s engines could power a drive—and there was a fully-equipped boat that was capable of reaching the nearer constellations; add one or two of the big engines to its sturdy hull and you would have a ship that could cross the galaxy.

Buchanan thought of Liz Deffant. And then of Kochan's granddaughter.

"Maran, do you know why I came here?" he said, his voice hollowly echoing around the inside of the helmet and setting up fresh echoes in the wreck of the liner.

"Yes," said Maran, and Buchanan saw his eyes, always estimating, always planning, full of awareness. "I know, Buchanan. You came to find why you failed."

"I didn't fail!"

"You failed."

"It was the robots!"

"No robot can defeat a determined man."

"They took the screens down—they let the *Altair Star* sink into *this*!" And Buchanan indicated the glittering, menacing tunnel where the lost ships eddied slowly.

"Order the machines to build a drive, and I'll tell you why you failed."

Buchanan felt a sense of helplessness. "You can't escape the cruisers."

"Buchanan, would it help if I said I believed that too?"

Buchanan could not face the self-questioning that stormed into his mind. He said quickly: "Yes, Maran!"

"Then I promise you, Buchanan, that I have every reason to believe escape from the Singularity impossible."

"Tell me. Where I failed. Why—*this*." And he gestured heavily to the gap beyond where the bridge had been, and where Preston had led the assault on the machines in the last vain effort to hold back the long night.

What did it matter that Maran should have a lifeboat, however powered? Buchanan had to know why the robots of the *Altair Star* had quietly surrendered seven hundred lives.

"The machines were faced with an anomaly," said Maran.

"I know that."

"Then you should have expected their reaction."

Buchanan thought of the last moments of the *Altair Star*. Think calmly, logically, coherently, at such a time? Yet he had done what he thought best. At the Court of Inquiry there had even been congratulations.

"That's all?"

"Buchanan, faced with the impossible, they decided that their function was at an end."

And then he could imagine the machines' calm decision—could almost hear their flat voices, almost see the relays flickering to the inevitable conclusion.

"They gave up because—"

"Because they decided that their context could not be, Buchanan. If their surroundings were becoming impossible, so were they!"

Buchanan repeated hollowly: "If their surroundings were impossible, so were they! Everything about them could not be—could not exist!—so they stopped!"

"Now you have it," said Maran. "Accept it."

"You didn't."

Maran was almost sympathetic. "I am Maran." He was silent for a moment, and then his voice boomed around the hulk: "Call to your machines, Buchanan."

Buchanan laughed. He had found Maran's weakness. The man had forgotten that the machines were outside the Quasi-warp's protective fields.

"You'll have to awaken the dead," he said. "Maran, how can I reach the memory-banks?"

"Watch!"

Maran spoke and the life-raft seemed to come alive. Its small engines jerked and thrashed at his commands, and the little vessel shivered as power screamed from its drive. Dazed by the blast which rocked the big liner's hulk, Buchanan became aware only gradually of the increasing strength of the Quasi-warp.

"Don't!" he yelled suddenly, aware that the tenuous glories of the eerie field were creeping beyond the space where the bridge had been.

"Maran—don't let it touch them!"

Horrified, he watched as the bizarre forces of time-locked tunnel and strange Quasi-warp met and merged. The strange warp began to invest more of the *Altair Star;* but Buchanan's eyes were riveted on the splayed, fresh bodies.

"It has to be done!" boomed Maran.

"But they—they're not dead!"

He would have hurled himself at Maran had he not been rendered stiff with fresh horror by the sight of the bodies; for, as the Quasi-warp reached them, merging with the tunnel's coruscating white-gold, the processes of death reasserted themselves; and Buchanan saw time run its course. The bodies decayed.

Preston was a ghastly gray-green sight, his handsome features billowing with mold; and, within seconds, the features had gone and only white bone remained. Time surged on and bone crumbled, turned to dust, was swept about in the gusting fields so powerfully countered by the combined drives of the station and the little raft. Buchanan breathed a prayer.

It was for himself. He did not want to think of what was happening throughout the lounges and private cabins of the *Altair Star*.

"They were always dead!" Maran snapped. "Buchanan, nothing can reverse death—nothing! It was held back, but that's all—there was never anything you could do for them!"

There was more than anxiety in his voice, Buchanan recognized; the man was oppressed by the aura of the doomed ship. The ghosts clamored throughout its deck, now released from some weird limbo that had held them, while outside, in the slowly wheeling Galaxy, three years had passed.

"Buchanan, order the machines to regard me as commander, and then return to the station!"

Buchanan moved ponderously toward the small dust-heaps. Why not help Maran? There was nothing he could do now for the *Altair Star*. Its frozen moment was over. Only he was left, after the passage of the years. The time-locked tunnel had released the undead. The fabric of its grotesque white-gold fields had been burst open. Why not let Maran get what he wanted from its depths?

He passed more heaps of dust where clusters of men and women had waited. Terrified groups, facing eternity together. He reached a master-console and was not even surprised when it glowed into life at his touch. He gave the brief instructions and returned.

"Ask Miss Deffant to watch," Maran said.

Watch what? But Buchanan did not care.

Maran moved decisively. He pointed to the battered raft, edging Buchanan toward the port. "Go back,

Buchanan. Go to Miss Deffant! Tell her Maran said she should watch!"

"I'll tell her," said Buchanan.

The last he saw of Maran was his broad back, unnaturally huge in the deep-space armor, radiant with the fires of the Quasi-warp.

CHAPTER 20

Liz Deffant saw the return of the life-raft with anguish. She rushed to the hold to see Buchanan, huge and armored against the gold-shot tiny black pits which opened in the fabric of the station. She waited as the robots took off his suit.

She knew that he had seen things too terrible to speak of.

"Come," she said.

Buchanan did not notice that she was unsurprised to see him return alone. She half pushed, half led him to the grav-chute and the cabin above. Only when they reached the bridge did Buchanan speak.

"Liz," he said with a disbelieving calm, "Liz, they were there. They were all there—in the ship."

"Later, Al," whispered Liz. "See!"

Buchanan automatically reached for sensor-pads as the big screen burst into life. Scanners roved; the screen pulsed, cleared, and settled. It was the *Altair Star*.

Buchanan and Liz Deffant were fascinated by the rippling, blinding, utterly *alien* surge of power as the massive engines of the ship began to weave the impossible, monstrous web of forces summoned into being by Maran's strange genius. They saw a great band of energies eerily combine to form a single Quasi-warp that pushed aside the eddying configurations of the time-locked tunnel.

"He's going," whispered Liz Deffant, but the words were barely audible, only a thin breathing, an automatic carry-over from a forgotten state of mind. The majesty of the thing she and Buchanan watched obliterated all else.

The big lifeboat of the *Altair Star* was the source of the Quasi-warp. It nosed out of the rent in the lost ship's side, and colossal shards of the strange tunnel gave way before it. The Quasi-warp bent the fabric of the tunnel.

The scanners held the terrible majesty of the scene. The

screen flowered with renewed violence; the lifeboat was a star-center. Waves of energies began to rock the station. Buchanan's hands shook.

His mind cleared at last. "Maran!" he said urgently. "He's using the boat to escape!"

It hadn't been at all important aboard the lost ship; but here, at the station, Buchanan was again a Galactic Service employee, responsible to the Council and aware of Maran's inexplicable and unholy powers.

Liz Deffant gripped his arm. "Al—watch!"

By her tone he knew that she was in possession of information he had missed. There was a resigned, sad tone in her voice that he recognized. He had no time to consider it, for the lifeboat became a blossoming cancer, white-gold in a sea of fragmented, blistered, impossibly complex black-lighted powers. The Quasi-warp was demolishing the entire time-locked tunnel.

From the center of the sea of black shards, the lifeboat rose up and hung, poised. The station was hurled away by the hurricane that was its wake. Yet the scanners kept to their task; Buchanan and Liz Deffant clearly saw the end of the *Altair Star*.

It was one of a score of ships that danced, whirled, and spun zanily in the wash set up by Maran's overpowered boat. The *Altair Star* lurched end over end. A tiny, ancient rocketship cannoned into it. Were its crew even now joining the ranks of the dead? It was a grotesque, fantastic sight; the thought of the crew of the ancient, tiny ship which had adventured so many centuries before across the gulfs, was strangely haunting. Other ships smashed into one another. Fragments of lost ships too joined the crazy corybantics set up by the Quasi-warp.

The two appalled watchers saw the lifeboat begin to surge forward, full of power. Blackness boiled around the wrecks. The Quasi-warp completed the destruction of the impossible tunnel that held them.

"He's going out!" Buchanan began to say. "Maran's—"

"No," said Liz, with a surprising harshness. "See!"

Buchanan looked into the depths behind what was left of the tunnel.

A blank, terrifying emptiness had opened at the core of the Singularity. Buchanan's thoughts spun. Somewhere among his memories was Maran's triumphant yell: *"An entire new Universe!"*

Was it?

It was a hole, a pit, a sink of energy, a nothingness, an alien and empty pathway of pure night, black and lost, blank and void.

The poised lifeboat seemed to hesitate.

"No!" Liz Deffant cried, responding to the eerie emptiness of the gaping pit. "No, Maran!"

Flooding with tendrils of white-gold glory, the great drive that had once powered the *Altair Star* built to a crescendo. The lifeboat pulsed, glowing, blasting, roaring forward, driven by the huge engines.

Straight into the black hole.

"Gone!" breathed Buchanan.

There was more to follow, equally strange.

"Dear God, the *Altair Star*!" Buchanan gasped.

He and Liz saw the ghost-fleet spin slowly around the wreckage of the time-locked tunnel. And then they resumed their interrupted voyages.

They were free of the grip of the bizarre enigma.

One by one, the long-lost ships followed the still-writhing wake of Maran's lifeboat. In a stately procession, like carriages in a funeral cortege, the ships descended into the terrible emptiness.

Buchanan was nerveless, stupefied.

He watched the end of the *Altair Star*. For seconds, it was outlined against the white-gold translucence, and then it was gone. The dust of so many human beings was on its way to the most weird interment ever known. The great infragalactic liner, at last, was gone.

"It's over," said Liz.

Buchanan felt a curious sense of relief. His ghosts were truly laid. And then he thought of Maran.

What strange Universe had received him!

"Maran?" he asked Liz.

"He left a message."

Together, they listened to the deep, powerful recorded voice: "Miss Deffant! Buchanan! The station is now yours. Maran will trouble you no longer. If Maran is wrong, he will trouble the Galaxy no more." There was a change of tone, and Buchanan sensed an edge of regret. No human being could renounce all he had known without some feeling of apprehension. "Maran recognized your nobility of spirit, Miss Deffant. Buchanan is a fortunate man. As for Maran, he will try to enter into the Universe he saw. It may be that in another kind of life, he will be able to continue his investigations into the greatest of all mysteries. For, make no mistake, the structure which exists in the Jansky Singularity is no accident! Maran recognizes the handiwork of an intelligent entity. So Maran leaves you and the Galaxy that rejected him to find beings capable of understanding his ambitions." Quietly, he added: "Think of Maran, Miss Deffant."

Buchanan shivered.

It was like listening to a recording of a dead man's words.

"It is all over," he said.

"Is it?" Liz asked.

"Yes! For us, yes!"

CHAPTER 21

Lientand saw that the station had suffered. Unguessable forces had eaten at its fabric. Whole sections had been smashed clear away. No darting scanners roamed before it. It was a blind, crippled, failing nugget of technology that had just managed to stagger clear of the appalling chaos within the Singularity. Nevertheless, helpless as the station appeared, Lientand kept his cruisers' main armament on it.

"Still no beamed transmissions, sir," reported his lieutenant. "The life-support systems are working, but there's not much power."

"Get him," said Lientand.

He wondered if he should risk his crew. His humanity struggled against a growing conviction that Maran should be put down as one would a mad dog.

A launch set out, but before it covered the short distance to the station, a port opened in the scarred side. The launch followed.

"Take no chances," ordered Lientand, when the raft was inboard.

Seconds passed and then slowly a crack appeared in the bent and burned life-raft. A small port swung aside.

Restraint tentacles, hand-weapons, blast-screens: all were ready.

Then a crewman yelled incredulously: "It's a woman!"

Lientand began to believe in miracles.

When he heard the uproar, Rosario crawled from his bed, to the accompaniment of robotic protest. He ignored it and dragged himself to the hold. All over the cruiser, men were roaring their delight.

Buchanan helped Liz out. When he saw the way she looked at the lean, craggy-faced man, Rosario shrugged regretfully and listened.

"Where's Maran?" asked Lientand.

Buchanan still looked dazed. "Maran chose to go into the Singularity."

Lientand knew shock when he saw it, but there had to be the few vital, immediate questions. Then, and for days later, Buchanan could only give an account of what he had seen—when trained interrogators began their subtle questioning to see what he knew of Maran's motives, he could do nothing to help shed light on the inexplicable dynamics of the bizarre genius.

Maran; the time-locked tunnel; the black pit; the failure of the robots when the *Altair Star* was lost. Buchanan sensed a connection, but it was one that eluded him for many days.

It was only when he was interviewed by Kochan that the moment of insight arrived.

No one else was present to hear Buchanan's appalling story. Kochan heard it all in silence, with hardly a change of expression on his wrinkled face. When Buchanan finished, he said: "You are quite sure about her?"

"Yes."

Kochan sighed. "I can live with it. Can you, Buchanan?"

"I think so."

There would be the sadness, the regret, the memories, but the dread was gone. Liz Deffant would be there.

"There'll be another station," said Kochan. "Bigger. You'll want it?"

"No."

"I'm interested in the Quasi-warp. There's a lot of work to be done at the Singularity."

"Not by me," said Buchanan. He thought of the impossible tunnel, the alien blackness. "I'm making a suggestion to the Council about it, sir."

"Investigation?"

"No."

"What then?"

"That we leave it alone."

Kochan's eyes did show emotion then. "Why?"

"I think we could become too interested in it. I also think it's too much for us."

"A mystery too deep for mere men?"

He thinks my nerve has failed, thought Buchanan. Kochan was not sneering, but the tone was sardonic.

Buchanan tried to explain: "You remember what Mrs. Blankfort said?"

"What was that?"

"She told me not to hate the robots."

"And?"

"I did. I loathed them for giving up the *Altair Star*."

Kochan was hostile now. "What point are you trying to make?"

"In a way," said Buchanan, aware of the hostility, "they were right."

"Right to abandon all hope—right to take my grandchild!"

"I used to think as you do."

"You've changed your mind. Why?"

"I believe the robots decided the Singularity was beyond our comprehension."

"It is!"

"But ours, sir," insisted Buchanan.

"Say what you mean."

"The robots believe we can't understand the Singularity —it's beyond us—beyond *us*—not beyond *them*!"

As he said it, Buchanan had a sudden vision of Maran at the console of the big lifeboat, pitching the overpowered little vessel into the frightful alien pit: Maran with his machines! Maran, striving to penetrate some vast mystery by offering himself up to the creatures that had built the time-locked tunnel.

"Go on," said Kochan.

Buchanan knew at last why the robots had surrendered his ship. Not because they believed the tunnel impossible. Maran had not told him the truth. The machines had wanted to keep the secret of the tunnel away from human beings.

"That's all there is, sir," he said helplessly. "I think the robots are right. They don't believe the human race ready for the forces loose in the Singularity. That's why they accepted the inevitability of the complete loss of ships that went near it. That's why the robot satellites were lost so soon. The robots kept us from the Singularity through fear."

"You came out. With the station."

"It took a Maran."

"Yes," said Kochan, and Buchanan sensed in him something of Maran's terrible simplicity. Kochan smiled. "You've done your part, Buchanan. You'll find me grateful."

Buchanan realized that Kochan had found a new goal. He intended that the Singularity should give up its secrets.

He hated it with a pathological anger. He wanted revenge on the monstrosity that had destroyed his grandchild. By plundering its fantastic recesses, he would be gaining some recompense for her loss.

Buchanan thought bleakly of the strange efflorescence that was the black hole. It was the ultimate danger. And Maran was in it. What would that bizarre genius work in the alien pit?

There was nothing he could do. Naturally he would point out the dangers. But men like Kochan inevitably would maneuver, scheme, fill others—like himself!—with a fiery passion to *know*, and then the window into that other Universe would be wrenched open by the might of the Quasi-warp.

"I've done my part," Buchanan agreed. He had fought his one and only campaign.

"Miss Deffant is waiting," said Kochan, not unkindly.

Buchanan knew that he had been dismissed. He thought with pleasure of the little survey-ship.

While the Galaxy lasted, he and Liz would do the necessary, useful things like surveying barely-known star-systems and bending plant-forms to new uses.

He went, for he and Liz had waited long enough.

Let those who could make the mind-reeling decisions.

Let those who dared enter the Jansky Singularity.